# Mojo Rising

# Mojo Rising

## Volume 2
## Contemporary Writers

Edited by
## Joseph B. Atkins

**Mojo Triangle™ Books**
an imprint of

SARTORIS
LITERARY
GROUP

A traditional publisher with a non-traditional approach to publishing

SARTORIS LITERARY GROUP
www.sartorisliterary.com

This book is dedicated to my 8th grade English teacher, William E. Watson, the first writer I ever knew, a great raconteur who taught us the wonders of books and literature, regaled us with tales by and about Edgar Allan Poe, Jack London and others, and made me want to be a writer.

# CONTENTS

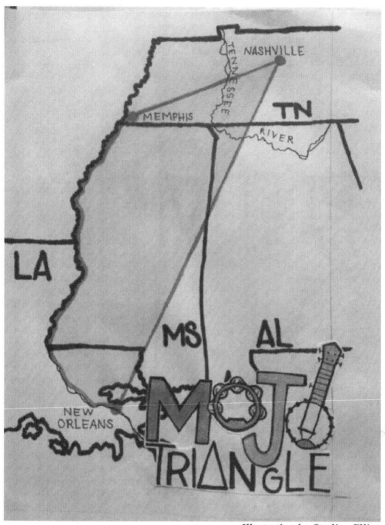

Illustration by Sterling Ellis

# What is the Mojo Triangle?

Draw a straight line from New Orleans to Nashville, then over to Memphis and back down to New Orleans following the curves of the Mississippi River, and you have the Mojo Triangle, a geometrical, cultural, and spiritual configuration that represents the geographical birthplace of America's original music—Country, Blues, Jazz, and Rock 'n' Roll—and the home of America's most powerful and innovative literature.

# INTRODUCTION

Edgar Allan Poe, my first literary hero as a 14-year-old would-be writer growing up in my corner of the U.S. South, believed the short story to be the ultimate expression of the literary arts, superior to the novel and even the poem because of its singular commitment to truth.

"The tale proper, in our opinion, affords unquestionably the fairest field for the exercise of the loftiest talent, which can be afforded by the wide domains of mere prose," wrote the author of "The Tell-Tale Heart", "The Pit and the Pendulum," "The Black Cat," and other bone-chilling tales that kept my teenage self awake at night.

Poe was a Virginian who, yes, had the Southerner's penchant for the arcane, the occult, macabre, and gothic but also for a certain, hard-gained truth. You still get hints of Poe in modern Southern writers like Sheree Renée Thomas, Jere Hoar, and Corey Mesler, all represented by stories in this anthology.

This Poe-like mélange is nowhere more evident than in the region of the Deep South we call the Mojo Triangle, which stretches from Nashville to Memphis down through the Mississippi Delta into New Orleans and then northward at an arc through central Mississippi and northern Alabama back into Nashville. This indeed is the fertile crescent of the larger South and the nation as a whole.

The music here speaks for itself—whether blues, jazz, rock 'n' roll, country, or rockabilly. Walter Anderson, William Eggleston, Theora Hamblett, and George E. Ohr, the "Mad Potter of Biloxi," stand shoulder-to-shoulder with the best artists, photographers and potters anywhere in America.

However, nowhere has the fertility of this Mojo land been more evident than in its literature. An accompanying volume to this one pays homage to the "old masters" such as William Faulkner, Eudora Welty, Tennessee Williams, and Richard Wright. This volume is living proof that Mojo soil is still the richest this side of the Nile, and come to think of it, the Mississippi River concedes nothing to the Nile, thank you very much.

A lot of struggle and suffering made this soil rich. Poverty, racial hatred, ignorance, intolerance, greed, isolationism, paternalism, Old Testament, Bible-thumping, foot-stomping fire-and-brimstoneism and First Baptist snobbism are all part of a rather unholy Mojo stew that would make even the witches in *Macbeth* turn their noses away. And let's not forget natural disasters—the yellow fever epidemic of 1878, the flood of 1927, and Hurricane Katrina in 2005.

Still, what great stuff for literature!

Of course, the Mojo Triangle isn't the only fertile patch across the global literary landscape. The Russians, led by the likes of Pushkin, Chekhov, and Gogol in the art of the short story, always demanded that fiction "be a true mirror of life and be of service to life," and thus writers do not look down upon the poor from a haughty distance, rather "from within, as one of them," and they see the poor "as human beings like the rest of us," literary editor Thomas Seltzer once wrote.

Yiddish literature, with its insistence on remembering

the lost world of the Eastern European "shtetl" and the demands of a God-haunted culture, reminds one of Mojo literature, where the village and small town still resonate even if only in the memories of city dwellers in Memphis and New Orleans.

"Although the short story is not in vogue nowadays," the great Yiddish writer Isaac Bashevis Singer said in 1981 about a condition which still holds true today, "I still believe that it constitutes the utmost challenge to the creative writer. Unlike the novel, which can absorb and even forgive lengthy digressions, flashbacks, and loose construction, the short story must aim directly at its climax. It must possess uninterrupted tension and suspense."

All good fiction, including the short story, "is unique and general, national and universal, realistic and mystical," Singer wrote.

This is a perfect description of the stories in this anthology.

Certainly the "mystical" is here. From voodoo in New Orleans to hoodoo in Memphis, this part of the South has always allowed a certain other worldliness to cohabitate with the often not-so-pleasant realities of this world. The young protagonist in Sheree Renée Thomas' "Aunt Dissy's Policy Dream Book" has to deal with the demanding reality that she possesses the "Sight" and all that it brings with it. Memphis conjureman Beaureguard Rawhead in Corey Mesler's "Conjuration: A Fabliau" wants to be a songwriter, and he's willing to give bluesman Tiny Red the love potion he seeks if Tiny will help him. In my own story, *The Singapore Holy Man*, a Russian émigré in Memphis, even after his death, manages to import some magic he found in Singapore.

Any discussion of post-mortal existence down here has to pay homage to Elvis Presley at some point. Those fans standing outside Graceland every day will tell you in a heart beat: the King not only lives on but will live forever.

One such fan, Elvis impersonator Aaron Rubens, shows us in writer and publisher James L. Dickerson's "The Second Coming" that Elvis may be still in the house in ways we never imagined.

Like most Mojo singers and musicians, Elvis was always singing about love and lost love, a theme that Mojo writers know well, too. Jere Hoar's "Prey Don't Tell" takes us to a zoo — of all places — to show us just how costly lost love can be. Love isn't just between a man and a woman. In Larry Brown's "Girl on the Road," young Fay escapes a loveless home to meet a couple trying to fill a void that love once filled. Three stories in this collection attest to a kind of "Long Lost Daddy" tradition in Southern storytelling. Margaret Skinner's "Lou Groza" and Steven Barthelme's "Coachwhip" provide psychic bookends to the volumes that could be written about encounters with the father who wasn't there and then abruptly is. In Maurice Carlos Ruffin's "Beg Borrow Steal," Pop finally comes back from prison but that means anything but smooth sailing ahead.

The world best knows William Faulkner, the lion of Mojo writing and perhaps all writing this side of the Atlantic, as a chronicler of a benighted South with its Sartorises, Snopeses, and black servants and sharecroppers sharing a disintegrating world. He was so much more, however. He and other gothic-prone Mojo storytellers like Elliott Chaze and Tennessee Williams could be every bit as hardboiled and noir as Dashiell Hammett, James Cain, and Raymond Chandler. That side of the Mojo tradition is represented well here by writers such as Ace Atkins, Julie Smith, and William Boyle, whose tales of old gumshoes, crooked cops, and small-time hustlers tell of a South that's more urban and scary with a dark undertow that constantly threatens. Still, even in the hot, sultry nights of that Mojo land can usually be found another Southern verity, retribution. It's as inevitable as the fragrance of magnolia and sweet taste of bourbon summer evenings on the porch.

So enjoy this assembly of Mojo writing, and with it rest assured the soil is indeed as deep and dark as ever down here. The South's not going anywhere. Why would it?

**--Joseph B. Atkins**

**Ace Atkins**

# LONG LAST RIDE OF EL CANEJO

## By ACE ATKINS

You got six months, probably less, and your wife asks you a simple question: What do you want to do with your time?

"Die?" you ask, grinning at her.

"We can go anywhere you like, you can get hospice anyplace."

"They shouldn't call it hospice," you say. "They should call it Die Son of a Bitch Die."

"It's your time. Do what you want."

And it's not a week later, that you're in the passenger seat of the Buick, always loving to drive, but the doctor saying it's not a good idea with all the painkillers and medications or horse pills and such. Your legs don't work so good either, now having to tool around in a wheelchair while the cancer goes to work on you. Throat cancer lighting up your hospital charts like a goddamn Christmas tree.

You decide to head south, back to the beach where you all started out after the war when you got out of the Navy. You moved down to Tampa, where you worked as a newspaperman and then a sheriff's detective, busting up moonshine stills and illegal gambling. Down here they called you *El Canejo*, the rabbit. You were known. You were famous.

You made the Mafia greaseballs shit themselves on occasions.

"Why don't you call up the old gang?" you ask.

"I think most of the old gang is dead," your wife says.

"What about Buddy?"

"We got a Christmas card."

"Still in Daytona Beach?" you ask.

She nods.

"Call him."

The wife has rented the condo for the month, a two-bedroom unit on the fourth floor. Sea Breeze 2. You gripe that it has a shit view, looking across the banyan trees and palmettos rooted in a little abandoned lot by the main road. You preferred something looking out at the Gulf.

"I can push you down to the dock," she says.

"And then I'm relying on you. I'd rather just be up here. I need a place to smoke."

"You've got to be kidding me."

"Yeah," you say. "It might kill me."

* * *

Your boys and daughter come to visit. And there isn't much crying and all that, because they know how much you hate that crap. You try to make jokes about getting sponge baths and the horse pills. You got two nurses, a fat black woman and old white woman who calls you captain.

You had been the captain of the vice squad back in the fifties, your wife had told them. Captain, she calls you.

The black woman carries a big black bag filled with nothing but bottles and vials and needles. One needle is as long as your forearm.

"What's that for?"

"Seizures."

"Calms them?"

"Mmm-hmm. Real Good."

About the only action in the whole condo — besides the eating and the talking and the dressing — comes from the maids. Man, how you do love the maids. They are from Eastern Europe someplace, young girls with good bodies and teeth, tanned and curvy and shy in that sexy kind of way. They don't look like maids.

You have never seen maids like that.

When they look at you, you wink and tip the brim of your Irish cap. One of them, a dark girl with a nice tan, winks back Man, that makes your day.

"Just why are they here?"

"Everyone needs a job," your wife says.

"With bodies like that, they don't need to be scrubbing toilets."

"They're nice girls."

"You see the fella who runs this place?" you ask.

"No."

"He's suspicious."

"Everybody is suspicious to you."

"He's mobbed up. You take my word for it. He's mobbed up."

"Why do you say that?"

"The Albanians and all that shit are running the show now," you say. "Don't you read the papers? All the old grease balls are dead. They don't have the stomach for it."

"Please don't embarrass me."

"Can I just make an observation?"

* * *

You start taking some pleasure in watching him. You learn his name is Fatmir. Which is pretty funny since he's bloated in the face and porky in the body and wears satin track suits and gold jewelry. You tell your wife that maybe he learned to dress like a mobster from watching American TV.

19

"Maybe he likes track suits."

"Yeah, he looks like the physical fitness type."

"You want something to eat?"

"Let's go down to the diner. What's that place called?"

"Pete's."

"Yeah, yeah."

"What're you thinking?" she asks.

"Ham and eggs."

"What are you thinking?"

"I used to run bastards like this."

"What has he done?"

"You bet your ass he's done something."

\* \* \*

You have that old white nurse wheel you out around the swimming pool and out to the pier and she's chattering on about the *blattedy-blah-blah* about the winter in Florida and how all her friends were jealous back in Buffalo or Cleveland or some place. And the thing about being old and dying is that you don't have to act like you give a rat's ass about any of it.

"Would you like something?"

"A cold beer," you say.

She laughs like it wasn't a real request and you wait till she's gone to turn down the oxygen tank and take off that fucking mask and light up a Backwoods cigar. You smoke it down a good halfway when you see Fatmir roll up in a metallic green Humvee with chrome wheels. Two girls are with him; one is the maid who winked at you and some other young good-lookin' gal.

They're not dressed as maids. They wear tight halter tops showing off belly rings and tight blue jeans with high heels and you roll forward a bit in the wheelchair staring through the open space of the parking garage facing the pool.

The girls, looking damn near identical, peel off a roll of

bills from tight jean pockets and hand over a cut.

They don't notice you.

When you're a decrepit old man, no one does. You kind of wished you'd had this disguise when you were busting up the old Bolita racket in Ybor City. Back then they saw you and Buddy and from a mile away, hearing Ires Canejos! Tres Canejos! The Cubans figuring if you were a rabbit, then your buddies were, too.

You wonder if you could still tap a phone line, thinking about it, till you spot Fatmir's fat ass pull out a cell phone from his track suit and make a call. So it's just surveillance. It was always just surveillance back then, too.

* * *

"You want me to turn on the TV, Dad?" your daughter asks.

"Fetch me a beer."

She doesn't give you shit. She's a good daughter and grabs a cold Budweiser. She props you up on a deck chair on the little balcony overlooking the vacant lot. She says her goodbye, a little teary eyed, and you promise not to die overnight if you can help it. And she grabs her keys to head back to the motel.

You don't feel so great. But you don't feel like you're dying. Maybe that's the bitch of the pills.

You doze off and wake up sometime in the middle of the night, maybe three in the morning. Two men are arguing in some foreign tongue down in that vacant lot among all the stunted trees and palmettos growing in that sandy soil. You spot their thick shapes in the moonlight and a flash of bright red from a jacket. They're carrying something heavy, bitching at each other in that foreign speak about who's holding the most weight, tossing what they got over a long wall made of cinder blocks.

21

One of the men disappears and then comes back with two shovels. It's windy up on the balcony and smells of saltwater and dead fish.

The men light up some cigarettes and rest, leaning against the wall. You run your hands over the wheels of your chair and roll forward, trying to be quiet and slow, but damn if you don't knock what's left of your warm beer through the balcony railing.

The men look up after the glass shatters.

Fatmir cranes his fat neck and has a good look at your face. He doesn't look happy.

\* \* \*

"Maybe they were fishing," your eldest son says.

"With shovels?

"Couldn't have been poles?

"I got cancer, not brain damage. Jesus."

"It's dark. Tough to see."

"When's Buddy coming?" you ask, yelling back to your wife. She's frying bacon and eggs, making coffee.

"Tomorrow."

"Get his ass on the phone."

\* \* \*

Buddy wears an orange-ish Hawaiian shirt with seagulls and palm trees and water and bullshit. You remember the time he got into a scrap with a greaseball heavy named Cowboy Ippolito and Buddy tossed him through a plate glass window. When was that? Fifty-eight?

He's grown fat and bald in the last fifty years.

"You look fat," you say.

"You gonna eat that?"

"No," you say. "Take it."

22

Buddy reaches for your bacon at Pete's diner, having wheeled you into the end of the booth. The anchor tattoo on his hairy forearm has faded a great deal.

"This place reminds me of that place? You know?"

"Ayres Diner," you say.

"Ayres Diner."

"Buddy, you bring a gun?"

"You said you wanted a .38."

"Where is it?"

"I don't have a .38."

"Couldn't you have brought any goddamn gun?"

"I don't want to be a part of what you got planned."

"Son of a bitch. You, too."

"Not like that."

"You think I'm gonna shoot myself?" you say. "Sheesh."

"What should I think?"

"This guy Fatmir wants me dead. I was watching the sunset last night and he comes over to me like we're old friends and puts his hands on the grips of my chair. He smelled like a dung heap. His breath like dead shrimp and cigarettes. "

"I can't believe it."

"Since when am I wrong about crooks?"

"I can't believe you watch sunsets."

"Bleh."

* * *

"Sweet mother of God," Buddy says.

You two are watching the sunset and drinking cold beer, a fishing pole in each of your hands. Buddy has turned away to watch two maids, different girls, ditch their working clothes for string bikinis and baby oil. One is blonde and the other brunette. They are tanned, narrow at the waist and curvy in the hip and ass.

"I'd like them to clean my toilet," you say.

23

"They speak English?"

"Does it matter?"

"You could bounce a ball off that woman's stomach."

"You could bounce a couple of 'em."

"You say they're whores?"

"Wait a second and they'll get a call. They always write something down, like an address, and take off real fast."

"Where's the big man?"

"He'll be around."

"Where's that hole he dug?"

"Shhh. Be quiet."

You reel in your hook and bait and see that the shrimp has been eaten away, leaving only an empty transparent head. "Son of a bitch."

* * *

"Are you scared?" Buddy asks that night, wheeling you down a sidewalk snaking along the main road from town, out of the cendo complex and down to the empty lot, separated with the wall of concrete blocks.

Lots of cars speed past you, blowing up grit and trash into your face, but you keep on rolling ahead. There is a single light up on a telephone pole, and out into the lot, you see a cat hopping around, trying to catch a lizard.

"He's gone. Don't worry."

"I mean about dying."

"Push me to the edge there."

"Can you walk at all?"

"Yeah, I just like you to push me around for fun."

"Are you scared?"

"I don't know, Buddy. Goddamnit. Over there, you see that?"

You point out a spot about three by six where the soil had been turned over. Buddy mops the sweat from his face and cleans his glasses with a clean handkerchief.

"I'm not afraid," Buddy says. "You want to know why?"

"Don't tell me you've gotten religion on me."

"It's the most important thing I've ever done," he says. "I haven't missed a Sunday in ten years."

"Bleh."

"Right there?" Buddy asks.

You hand him the shovel and point. "Come on. Come on."

\* \* \*

The cop is green as goose shit. He's young with a hairless face and a two-dollar haircut. You asked for a detective and you get a kid on traffic duty, taking notes on a fucking computer instead of writing stuff down for a man. It's nearly midnight before he shows up.

"Something funny?" he asks.

"Just never seen anyone take a report that way."

"I can file it by pushing a button."

"So this is just a report? I asked for a detective."

"Yes, sir."

"They buried someone back there."

"Where you found the bottle."

"The bottle had a note inside."

"And what did it say?"

"What did it say, Buddy?"

"It says mascara," Buddy says.

"And you know what that means, kid?" you ask the boy on patrol. His fingers stop typing. He drops his eyes, looking down from where he set up on the trunk of his cruiser. "It means asshole in Albanian," you say. "Look it up. Hey, they moved the goddamn body."

"Is there a bathroom around here?"

You toss your thumb over your shoulder at the toilets by the pool.

Buddy watches you open up the patrol car and look

25

around, giving a low whistle, reaching into the front seat. Buddy taps your shoulder as he spots the boy corning back, zipping up his fly.

You close the front door. The boy studies you.

"Hell of a machine. Me and Buddy were cops way back when."

"I think I got what I needed," he says, reaching for the door handle. "Thanks."

He drives slow down the condo parking lot and turns on the signal to make a turn.

* * *

Your wife picks up two T-bone steak dinners the next day from a place in Clearwater. They look and taste like elephant ears and the medication is making you nauseous. Early evening is slow; the kids have flown home. Buddy is gone, gripping your hand for a long time, crying a bit, telling you he'd try and stop by before you left.

Hospice has bathed and dressed you earlier, piling you into two thick shirts as you requested because it makes your bony frame fill out and because it feels so damn cold all the time. You add the Irish cap.

"You want dessert?" your wife asks.

"He wouldn't even get me a piece."

"A what?"

"A gun."

"We have ice cream."

You shrug. "It was nice to see the kids," you say.

You two eat ice cream in silence so damn still that you hear each scrape of the spoon.

* * *

She's left you to smoke a Backwoods cigar at the pier, promising to return after a quick trip to the grocery store. It's late, maybe seven o'clock at night, and the sun is long since gone and the only show comes from some ratty pelicans trying to sleep on the pilings. There's a speedboat some asshole had tied up where you like to fish and your eyes grow heavy as the hull slaps up and down in small waves.

You dream you are alone, detached and drifting, nothing but water and fog around you until you're back in that '54 Ford unmarked unit running wires off telephone lines listening in on Charlie Wall dropping the dime on grease balls before he got his throat cut, or parked outside Santo Trafficante's ranch house in Palma Ceia before he escaped to Cuba to run Havana with Meyer Lansky.

You smoke cigarettes, drink Old Forester in the old sheriff's office in the jail by the city graveyard. Your short-sleeved dress shirts and pants are pressed and your wingtips shine. You wear a .38 Chief's Special on your hip when you make those midnight meetings with Pelusa Joe at that old kiddie park, Fairyland, talking about the old Italians pushing out all the Spaniards and Cubans, blood wars heating up over gambling and bootlegging.

You feel as light as a goddamn balloon.

A girl cries.

You open your eyes and the whole damn scene doesn't seem real to you. All that fog and floating made sense, and then you get mad a little, knowing it was the meds making you go nuts.

You wheel yourself over to the woman sitting on the edge of the diving board. Her long tan legs are knocked together at the knee below a miniskirt. Her head is in her hands with hair spilling down in her face.

"You okay?"

She looks up and you expect her to be prettier. Her face is a goddamn mess. Split lip, eyes busted. Her arms and neck are bruised. Her face is wet from the crying and blood and she pats a paper towel to the marks. You figure the guy was wearing a ring.

"You speak English?" you ask.

She nods.

"Fatmir?

She nods.

"I saw you with another girl," you say. "She looked like you."

She says it was her sister.

"What happened to her?"

"Who are you?"

"I used to be a cop."

She nods.

"What happened to her?" you ask.

And she tells you.

Six girls brought in from the old country. They scrub toilets and screw men until they pay off Fatmir. The girl who'd winked at you had gone off the plan and Fatmir choked her out while polishing the bastard's nob.

There are five girls left and all of 'em scared shitless.

They can't go to the cops. The girl says home is even worse.

There's more. But it boils down to Fatmir being a first-class shitbag.

*  *  *

You feel like a million bucks as hospice bathes and dresses you early the next morning, buttoning you up in pajamas and placing your meds in a paper cup. They've started to corrode your insides, giving you some bad indigestion at night, and you ask what if you skipped them for now.

"The pain will be something else," the black nurse says.

"You won't be able to focus, enjoy the time you have," says the white nurse.

You take the pills with some bad Florida water. They set you into your wheelchair, spiffy and clean and ready for presentation. The black nurse has left her black bag open, that big ole horse needle sticking out of the top.

* * *

"Have I been a pain in the ass?"

"When?" your wife asks.

"Always."

"Pretty much."

Both of you sit at the condo kitchen table. She's signing thank you letters for all the cards and gifts you've been getting.

"But you love me?" you ask.

"Don't be silly."

"Me, too."

"I haven't been a pain in the ass," she says.

"Hah."

"What do you want to do tonight?

"Get drunk, go dancing. Stay up all night."

"Order in?"

"You wheel me down ?"

"The pier again?"

"Nice sunset."

"What did they do with my husband?"

"I like the colors."

"How corny," she says.

* * *

Fatmir wheels in that big green Hummer about an hour later, strutting out in a black muscle shirt and big puffy pants and sneakers. He's unshaven and fat and wears a lot of gold. At the edge of the parking lot, he lights a cigarette and begins to urinate against a fence.

He checks his watch, punches some numbers on his phone

with both hands, still pissing, and starts to talk. You move the wheelchair back from the light, shadowed in the edge of the parking garage, under a tennis court. A ball thwacks and pops above you. The wind off the Gulf is cold but smells like summer.

Fatmir starts to yell and puts the phone back in his pocket, looking up to the fifth floor and cursing for someone. He curses some more and heads to the elevators just as you wheel out into the wide parking lot and find the passenger door of the Hummer, staring up at the chrome handle as it were the moon itself.

That goddamn door handle is a mile away and it takes about every inch of you, your spine cracking as you stretch, to reach it and push, unlatching the door, finding purchase on the armrest and pulling yourself up and into the car. The girls have to work for him for two years or they get shipped back. There's other stuff, expected stuff, like drugs and pornography. Most of the money getting rolled in real estate, the same as the Italians did over on Treasure Island and Pass-A-Grille fifty years ago.

You make it halfway, your chest against the seat, your old useless legs hanging out into the window, wheelchair knocked down and away, hoping he can't hear shit from five stories up. But you finally right yourself, sweating and nearly passing out, trying to catch your breath like a beached fish, hands jittery, and spitting up blood into your fist.

You're fucked now.

You lean your head hack into the headrest, steadying your hands into the leather jacket over your pajamas. You've worn your Irish cap down in your eyes and you like the look of yourself staring into the rearview and then up to the fifth floor where Fatmir heads out from a condo and back to the elevator. You nod as you wait, wondering if he'll see your wheel chair toppled over into the empty parking space.

But he's a dumbshit, and a minute later, Fatmir jerks open

the door and jumps inside, breathing heavy and sweating, and it's a solid couple beats before he notices the old man in the pajamas sitting beside him.

Out of habit, he puts the key into the ignition. And that's when you lash out at the son of a bitch, stabbing him hard in the neck with the horse needle you stole and dropping that plunger down with your thumb. Fatmir holds his neck and screams at you, touching the blood in his neck and wanting to know what you've done.

You take that moment to snatch up his right wrist and click on the cuffs you stole from the patrolmen. You click the other end of the steering wheel.

He can't believe it. He can't fucking believe it.

You wink at him. *Goddamn, you're having fun.*

Whatever was in the needle has gone to work. You reach for the keys and crank the ignition, the big engine coming to life. He flops his fat head against the seat and lolls sideways, eyes wavering but on you. The windshield is wild and brilliant with gold and purple and blackness edging the horizon. You think it's a shame that the pretty scenes are wasted on the assholes of this world.

You knock the car into drive and use both hands to move your foot to the pedal, pressing down with all you got onto your left knee, the big sonofabitch Hummer heading through the parking garage, out the exit, busting through a wooden fence and across the polished pool deck. The light is so damn bright that you have to squint to steer, Fatmir's big shoulder rolling against you as the wheels bump and shutter over the path, crashing down the concrete steps and heading flat out onto the wooden pier.

That light so gold and bright, blue and black, that all of it the sea and earth and air looks like one goddamn thing.

The crash into the Gulf takes a lot out of you, the inch of wind you got in your lungs gone for a good long while. But you recover, pushing Fatmir against the driver's window that's half covered in seawater, the shiny hood nosing down, currents pulling you along.

You've brought your last Backwoods cigar for such an occasion and light it up with a Bic, making a show of blowing the smoke into the man's unshaven face. Water rushes at your feet and through cracks in the back windows.

Fatmir isn't talking.

"Look at those goddamn colors," you say.

"Why," he asks. "What does it matter?"

"Bleh," you say, water edging your chin and the orange tip of your cheap cigar. "It matters."

***

"The Long Last Ride of el Canejo" by Ace Atkins originally appeared in *Damn Near Dead 2*, published by Busted Flush Press. It is reprinted here with permission of the author, © Carrefour, Ltd.

Ace Atkins is the *New York Times* Bestselling author of twenty-one novels, including *The Fallen* and *Robert B. Parker's Little White Lies*, both out from G.P. Putnam's Sons in 2017. One of the best crime writers working today, Ace has been nominated for every major award in crime fiction, including the Edgar three times, twice for novels about former U.S. Army Ranger Quinn Colson. A former newspaper reporter and SEC football player, Ace also writes essays and investigative pieces for several national magazines including *Outside* and *Garden & Gun*. The Alabama native lives with his family in Oxford, Mississippi, where he's friend to many dogs and several bartenders.

**Maurice Carlos Ruffin**

# BEG BORROW STEAL

## BY MAURICE CARLOS RUFFIN

The first thing Pop do when he get home from Angola Prison is shove you and your little sister out the front door. He don't even say hi. He just tell Mama to please give him a dollar for you to get huckabucks. Mama tell him he got nerve telling her what to do with her dollar when she been trying to pay the bills all by herself for twenty-three and a half months and five days. The lights been out since last night, so how about earning a dollar? That one vein in the crook of Pop elbow pulse like a fat worm. He say you know I love you, baby. He push past Mama, borrow a five from her purse, and tell you not to come back till the street lights light up. You and Timithea head over to the Johnson's who sell chips, cold drinks, and everything on weekends, but the back window down and the curtains drawn, too, so they ain't open. Before long you and Timithea end up where the community center was before it burned. Full dump trucks wait like big, dumb elephants. You never do get those huckabucks.

When you come back, you and Timithea sit on the back porch floor and watch boxcars clank together. Timithea's hair barrette done fell loose, and you don't know how to fix it so you throw down your bouncy ball and let her chase it. She a lot more fun now that she more than a honeydew melon wrapped in swaddling. Even more fun than that mutt dog you had for a day that one time.

Pop open the back door, run his hand over your head, and say we going. You ask where. Mama smiling, and that make you smile...

Just do what you told, she say. But she don't say it mean. Pop grab Mama necklace.

Where the rest of that good jewelry I got you? Mama say she sold it all. She pick up Timithea and do that thing with her hand to check Timithea diaper like checking a pear to see if it taste good.

Pop whistle as we walk from the back yard to the front of the house. He toss the keys at you.

You want to drive? He ask.

Serious? You ask.

It's Mama car that she bought with her own money. The thing got a spoiler on the back hatch and pink dice hanging like cherries from the mirror. She don't even like Pop driving it, but maybe everything different now.

Fight me for it, he say. We wrestle on our feet, laughing the whole time. He put you in a headlock, but you hold that key tight in your fist.

But when you get behind the wheel, he shaking his head.

Get out, he say.

Why?

I thought you be taller by now. Instead, you just got fat. Your feet barely come down to the floorboard.

You don't move, but just keep your hands on the wheel. A bug crash into the front glass. It flutter for a sec like it's trying to figure what the shit just happen. Then the bug spin away.

Just around the block, you say. Pop smack the back of your head hard enough to make you fuzzy.

I don't have time for game playing. You think I'm about to go to back to that cage on account of letting a ten-year old drive?

35

\* \* \*

Pop drive you to a couple of places round town. First, to the supermarket where lobsters chop at the glass tank like they saying help man get me out of this place. The manager there know Pop and say he can't take on no felon. That ain't him. That's policy from on high.

Then Pop drive to the used tire garage, but the men there don't even let you get out the car. They bang on the hood and tell Pop to get ghost before they bust him in the mouth. One of the men come over to Pop open window. He got one gold tooth, but the tooth next to it missing.

I'd cap you right now if your offspring wasn't with you, the man say. He kick the car door, and Pop shout, but we drive away.

You go to Robinson Pizza under the highway bridge. Inside, Mr. Robinson come out from behind the counter. Something crawl by, and Mr. Robinson step on it. He see Pop and throw his hands up.

I don't want no trouble, Timmy, Mr. Robinson say. Pop frown at Mr. Robinson. Then Mr. Robinson tap him on the jaw real light. They hug. Pop say something in Mr. Robinson ear. Mr. Robinson slap Pop back and tell you hey little Tim you gonna be a sumo wrestler one day.

I need to make some money, Pop say. Lights due. Rent due. Life due.

Kitchen Sink Tyrone got sent to federal lockup in Mississippi, Mr. Robinson say. And nobody ain't seen Jupe since Christmas. Jupe was Pop best friend. The last time you saw him he and Pop showed you how to crack open a steering wheel column and hot wire a car.

No, Pop say, not that kind of money. Mr. Robinson raise his eyebrow.

You for real?

Can't a man change his hustle? I want to pay taxes and

shit. Is that wrong? If I could sell my blood, I would, but I ain't got that much blood. You feel me? Mr. Robinson pinch Pop shoulder and wink at you.

Your old man growing up, son.

* * *

Pop can cook, but Mr. Robinson kitchen full up. That's why you and Pop riding up the avenue to where all the white college dorms at. You got hot pizza and breadsticks on your lap. You want to reach in and grab a bite of something, so you reach in and pinch a hunk of pineapple and anchovies. Who the shit order pineapple and anchovies? You don't want Pop to see what you did so you eat the nasty stuff. It burn the roof of your mouth. Pop stuck a Robinson Pizza sign on the roof of Mama car. The sign keep slapping the roof. Wuk. Wuk. Wuk. The back of your head still hurt. Now your mouth hurt, too, and your stomach gurgling from the poison.

Pop park by a big house with symbols on the front you can't read. Make you feel stupid, and you don't like that feeling, so you make up a meaning for them. Crazy White People Here.

A boy with a belt wrapped round his head answer the door. He call back for somebody name of Charlie and a white girl come to the door. A white girl name of Charlie, but who look like a Charlene or whatever white girl's names be. Her eyes open, but she looking woozy like she dreaming on her feet.

Hold it, Mr. Bill Cosby, she say real slow. I have to give you a proper pourboire. Somebody in the house yell out what no Jell-O pudding pops? The girl flip through some money and count off dollars one-by-one all the way to seventeen. She shut the door. Pop grin.

That's an alright tip, he say. Then he yell. What you doing by my car?

There's a white boy in a baseball cap sitting in the driver

seat. He crank the engine, and the back tire spin before the car move. Pop a fast runner, but he only get a little way down the street before Mama car out of reach.

* * *

At the police station, Pop talk to a cop for a while. You don't like being in the station, but Pop say it's about time the cops do something to help him for a change. A skinny cop at the desk tell him they'll look into it, but don't get his hopes up. A man in a black suit call Pop name. The man look like a funeral man. Pop don't look him in the eye.

I didn't expect to see you back here so soon, Funeral Man say. You people just can't fly right, can you?

Pop tell him about the car. Funeral Man snort.

Well, was it retaliation? What did you do steal from them?

I ain't got to take this, Pop say, and pull you up from the chair you sitting on.

You'll take what I give you, Funeral Man say. Causing trouble is a violation of your parole. I can have you back in central lock up before your kid bellies up for fried chicken tonight.

Outside, Pop walk away from the station real quick. You get out of breath trying to keep up, and you can't. His legs too long. Your legs too short. He stop around the corner and shove the meaty part of his hands in eyes.

You shoulda punched him, you say.

You think I deserved to go away like I did? To prison?

No, Pop. They did you wrong 'cause they could.

I did me wrong, he say. Don't be a dummy. You know I stole stuff. They didn't even get me for half what I took.

But you just borrowed that, you say. Pop told you a long time ago the difference between borrowing and stealing. Thieves steal cause they heartless and like to hurt people. Good people like him borrow because they need it more than who they taking from. Good people give to others like Pop gave all that jewelry to Mama.

I took a ring, Pop say. A real pretty ring with emeralds set in the side for your Mama, but lost it running away that night they got me. I did what I did and took my lick. But I need you to listen to me. You listening? Just because I messed up don't mean I can't be somebody else now.

\* \* \*

It's a long walk from the police station to the horse racetrack, but you get there fast. Chop Shop Alley Pop call it. A bunch of garages lined up shoulder to shoulder. This was Pop and Jupe hangout spot. Two dudes talk by the garage farthest down. One of them is a white boy, Baseball Cap. Pop start running, but you trip on the gravel. When you get up, Pop holding the other dude by the arm, but Mama car gone again. Pop ask the dude where Baseball Cap live.

Who? The guy say and shrug Pop hand off his arm.

Why you playing stupid? Pop ask. The cat you was just talking to.

Him? I don't know him. He asked if I had a lighter, but I don't smoke.

\* \* \*

Your feet tired from all the walking. You been walking since Christmas it seem.

Maybe he already gave it to another chop shop, you say. Maybe we just too late. Maybe we should just go tell Mama. She might —

Pop pop you in the back of the head again. Everything fuzzy for a bit, but you don't stop walking.

You better not cry, Pop say. And even though your eyes want to let go, you don't cry. Pop put an arm around your shoulder. He rub the side of your head.

I don't mean to do that so hard, he say. Let's go in there. You go into a restaurant and Pop order ribs and Cokes, and you tear those ribs up quick, eat some greens, and wash it all down. The table next to you full of people like a family reunion or something. They waitress bring out a big cart of desserts with dishes of bread pudding and pecan pie. Some of that would set the pounding in your head straight, but you know better than to ask for dessert.

After more walking, you almost home. A block party happening and cars are parked all around. Fancy cars with fancy rims. Hoopties with garbage bags over the back windows. Pickups. Station wagons. It's like every car in the world here.

A few blocks away in front of a liquor store, there's a car kind of like Mama's. Only it's newer, and the tires shiny like they was just washed. Pop go to the car and graze the window with his hand like he stroking a kitten.

\* \* \*

Mama ain't happy about what happen with her car, and she ask what kind of man get home from prison for not even a whole day and manage to make things worse. She say she can't live like this. Pop sit at the kitchen table, next to a candle, with his hand over his eyes.

Timithea crying cause she hate the dark. You hate the dark, too, but you hate how hot it is with no AC even more. A light glow into your room from outside. The family next door TV on, and light and laughing come through your window from they window. You get up. You get the rod and screwdriver you keep under your bed and climb out the window. On the way down, your shirt tear on the hurricane fence, and you know Mama gonna kill you for ruining good clothes, but you about to make it up.

You walk back to where that look-alike car was, and it's still there. You slide the rod into the gap between the window and the door. You feel the rod catch like you found the lock, but the door don't come open. You push the rod deeper.

Nothing move. You check, but nobody watching you. A car with a broken window worth almost as much as a normal one. You find a brick on the street. The brick heavy enough to break the window without even throwing it hard. But you pull the door and it open. You jam the screwdriver into the steering wheel column and something give.

\* \* \*

"Beg Borrow Steal" by Maurice Carlos Ruffin was originally published in *Kenyon Review* online and is reprinted with permission of the author. Maurice Carlos Ruffin's work has appeared in *Unfathomable City: a New Orleans atlas* edited by Rebecca Solnit and Rebecca Snedecker, *AGNI, Kenyon Review, Callaloo, Massachusetts Review, LitHub*, and *Virginia Quarterly Review*. He is the winner of the Iowa Review Fiction Award, the So to Speak Journal Short Story Award and the William Faulkner Competition for Novel in Progress. He is also a member of the Peauxdunque Writers Alliance and the Melanated Writers Collective. Maurice's first novel will be published by One World/Random House in 2019.

Steven Barthelme

# COACHWHIP

## BY STEVEN BARTHELME

They were both dead drunk. It had all started inside, the guy had been riding him, talking trash, and then Mitchell began to remember, it was like a procession, people he didn't much like, people who had given him a hard time, guy named Jeff at school, that must've been grammar school, and Robin, and that guy at that sad little dinner party in Boston, who hated Southerners and out of nowhere said, "Yeah, Texas is hell" and wanted to "go outside," the morons always want to "go outside," so this time he had gone, and some women, too, the big one who said, "He can talk," and others, and that's how he'd gotten out here in this oily Fort Worth parking lot behind the bar, the blacktop broken but glistening in the city lights from beyond this ditch or whatever it was, the night wind blowing grit into his eyes, and his nose bloody, kneeling on this guy in the plaid cowboy shirt, watching the loudmouth's eyes roll back, and his hands tight on the guy's neck, he was hardly resisting at all anymore.

I'm really no good at this, Mitchell thought--a lucky punch had put the guy down — he sort of stepped into it, shit, this is easy, no wonder they like it so much, I'm going to kill this fucker.

But Mitchell wasn't paying attention. He felt like puking, and his eyes were closing, and his mind was wandering, to a day he had spent with his father--Quinn, his real father—twelve years earlier. He hated his father. Even when his father died, he had not stopped hating him, but only thought, She didn't need fancy doctors to tell him that, when they discovered that his heart had a hole in it. His father had been 45.

* * *

They found the snake in August in a pile of stones in the only shade near a dry creek bed, long and white, lying oddly still, almost stunned, in the midst of big white blocks of limestone. Coachwhip, Quinn thought, and although he knew what it was, he told Mitch to get the book from the car. "We'll look it up," he said. "Watch the barbed wire. Bring the pillowcase, too."

It hadn't been hard to catch. Quinn had gotten his foot on it quickly, before it knew it was prey, or slow maybe from the heat. He'd never seen a slow Coachwhip, except ones that had been in cages for years and had no place to go.

Quinn sat on one of the rocks, holding the snake behind its head. It was about two and a half feet, a young one. Light, the color of sand, but Coachwhips varied a lot; some were red. Looking around at the bleached limestone the creek had cut its bed through, it was obvious why this one was almost white.

Mitch came back from the road.

"What've we got?" Quinn said.

"Just a minute," the boy said. He was sitting on the ground with his short legs splayed out to the black cowboy boots Quinn had bought for him. The boots looked ridiculously large, even though the boy was fat. He hadn't wanted boots, but Quinn had insisted. Got to have boots if we're going snake-hunting next summer.

"Look under 'Racers'," Quinn said. "Or *Masticophis*." Now he was showing off. Jesus, the Latin name, no less.

The boy noticed. His expression changed, some of the joy

went out of it. "You're teaching me," he said. His eyes had gone to slits. His too round face didn't look angry; he just looked like someone else's kid.

"Somebody's got to. Teach you, I mean. C'mon, what is it?"

"It's a Racer?"

"No, but you're close," Quinn said. "Did you find the pictures? Find the pictures."

The boy was back to tearing pages as he flipped through the *Field Guide* in his lap. He brushed the sweat from his forehead with his sleeve. They're so forgiving, Quinn thought. He's already forgiven me.

"Here it is!" Mitch said. "Lemme see it."

Quinn held the snake out to him, and it started to move again, but he tightened his grip.

"Western Coachwhip," the boy said, and then looked down at the color plates in the book again. "Maybe it's Eastern Coachwhip."

"They have maps in the back," Quinn told him. "They show you where each kind lives." When he heard a car, he glanced up, over the rocks and past the mesquite tree by the little creek, toward the road, but it was just a pickup.

When Mitch had checked the ranges of the two varieties and decided — Western — he looked up again. "I can keep him, Daddy?" And then, when he saw his father's hesitation: "You want him?"

Quinn laughed, involuntarily, and shook his head. "No." He shook his head again. "I was just thinking maybe it'd be better to let him go. You know, sometimes they die, you put them in a cage." But he felt uncomfortable, telling the boy he couldn't have what he wanted, and he tried to find some feeling behind the words, but all he thought was, Sometimes they die when a car runs over them, sometimes they die when a hawk catches them, sometimes . . .

"I can keep him, then?" Mitch said. "I'll take good care of

him. He won't die."

"Before winter," Quinn said, "you have to let him go. He won't make it through the winter."

The boy's nod, as he reached for the snake, was so slight that Quinn wasn't sure he'd even seen it.

"Mitchell?"

"Okay," the boy said.

"October first. And here. We'll come out here and let him go. Okay?"

"All right."

With luck, Quinn thought, it'll make it to October. And they walked back to the car.

\* \* \*

Son of a bitch used to come by once a week, or once a month, and pretend to be my father. Teach me things. He was a Boy Scout all right.

The guy in the cowboy shirt started to rise, brought a hand around and caught Mitchell's ear so hard he thought he was going to black out, and he slammed the guy's head back down against the blacktop. "Fucker," he said. "You miserable drunken slut." He held the cowboy's head down against the pavement, but the man was still.

If I kill him, Mitchell thought, they'll put me in Huntsville, I'm not rich enough to get out of it. He felt weak, and tired. His ear hurt. I shouldn't drink, he thought, not so much. We took the snake back and put it in that aquarium. It died, later. Never took me to let it go. He was afraid of me.

\* \* \*

Joanne was waiting in the front yard, pretending to be watering, but Quinn knew that she was there because they were late, so he was surprised she didn't complain, about the time or even about the child's new pet. Instead she asked him in.

"Stewart?" Quinn said.

"He's not here," she said, shutting off the hose. She was wearing sandals, and a light cotton dress, busy, blue marked with black.

She had moved in with somebody, but not until five years after the divorce, and by that time they had developed an easy friendship, so that she would say, We had a miserable marriage, but a happy divorce. Stewart did something with computers and telephone systems. In the wide, light living room, Quinn settled opposite her, on the arm of a big off-white armchair. She was sitting on a couch.

"You're sure it's not dangerous?" she said, when Mitch had disappeared into the back of the house with the snake.

Quinn shook his head. "If it bites him, put some peroxide on it. Just like any other scratch."

"Well, maybe he'll learn some responsibility," she said.

Quinn looked at the carpet. "Jesus, I wouldn't want to be a kid again. Always getting taught stuff."

She looked at him.

"I didn't mean anything by it," he said.

Her silence was worse, he thought, than any of the things he was imagining her saying, things about responsibility, about his being still more kid than man, about what he should be doing for his child that Stewart was now doing and how good Stewart was at it.

"I just meant that sometimes I wonder whether what I'm teaching him is right."

"You have the leisure," she said. Then she looked down. "I'm sorry. I wanted to talk to you, I really did. And now we've gotten into this. It was a rotten thing to say. I'm sorry." She shrugged, and showed him her open hands.

"None taken," he said, and took her hand, releasing it quickly. "It's just talk. Relax."

"Tell me something, Quinn," she said, and looked away. "When you were... when you used to sleep with Marianne and come home to me, how did you feel about me? I mean, did you—" She smiled. "I don't know what I mean."

"You mean Stewart is . . ."

She shook her head, slowly, and her look was tentative, wary. "Me," she said, and looked up.

"You want an answer?" He waited for her to nod, but she didn't, just kept staring, so he looked away. "Well, it's not very useful, but what I felt was--I loved you both." He smiled. "I still love you. Don't know where she is. So it goes, I guess."

"You're right. It's not very useful." The boy said something, from the back, coming down the hall toward the living room. Outside it was beginning to get dark. She looked toward the hall. "Stewart is sweet," she said.

Quinn rolled his eyes at her.

\* \* \*

Mitchell got up. Some kid came out of a door in the back of the dark bar, carrying a silver tub, poured it out, looked at them, walked back inside. The cowboy opened his eyes and got up on his elbows, then his knees, then stood.

Mitchell looked at him, vague, uncertain, and then he stopped caring. The cowboy began swinging, hitting him, first softly, clumsily, and then, when Mitchell just stood with his arms hanging, harder and harder until Mitchell's cheek was cut below his eye and his nose was gushing blood and he wobbled and then fell. The cowboy spit. No wonder they like it so much, Mitchell thought. It's easy. He was afraid I wouldn't like him. Didn't know what he was doing. He didn't have a clue. And then he died. Mitchell smiled, and closed his eyes. That must've come as a shock.

\* \* \*

"Coachwhip," © Steven Barthelme, originally appeared in *Columbia* magazine and is published here with permission of the author. Steven Barthelme has published four books and more than 120 stories, essays, and poems in *The Atlantic* and *The Atlantic.com*, *New Yorker*, *Esquire* online, *Yale Review*, *Southern Review*, *McSweeney's*, *Oxford American*, *New York Times*, *Los Angeles Times*, *Washington Post* and fifty other magazines and newspapers.

His work has won the Transatlantic Review Award, the Hemingway Short Story Award, two awards from the Texas Institute of Letters, among others, and two stories have been reprinted in the Pushcart Prize anthologies. His most recent short story collection is *Hush Hush* (Melville House, NY, 2012). In May 2017, he retired as director of the Center for Writers at the University of Southern Mississippi after 30 years at the university. He is editor of *Mississippi Review*.

Margaret Skinner

# LOU GROZA

## BY MARGARET SKINNER

My old man is Charlie Bill Stone. I call him Charlie Bill the same as the rest of his acquaintances down at Alex's where he drinks beer. That's the way he thinks of me, just an acquaintance. My wife, Annie, says stop following him around.

"Search for the *father*," she calls it. "Face up to it. He must have heard she had a baby — must have at least *thought* it might be his."

My mother had an affair with him, but called it quits and soon after married another man. Of my father, she said, "Once he started traveling, he never came around again."

Down at Alex's I sit near him and listen to his stories. I collect each anecdote and seal it into my memory, each word of him. He doesn't know me — the genetic affiliation, that is, and I find the whole secret irresistible — like colorizing an old movie, knowing full well that it ought to be left alone.

He didn't start out selling battery chargers. The job came up along with a freak of nature while he was peddling Rising Sun Flour in and around Memphis.

He didn't have to travel any further than Blytheville, Arkansas, or Greenwood, Mississippi, with the flour. Anyhow, it was then that he ran into Mr. Brock, the Everall

man.    Mr. Brock saw that he had mechanical ability right
away — Charlie Bill jump-started him in a snowstorm.

It happened on St. Patrick's Day when everything's supposed to be green.    Winter sometimes sits around Memphis
doing much of nothing, then, when it's time to move on,
shows off with a little going-away party.

Charlie Bill was sitting at the bar in Alex's with some
other men when snow started pouring from the sky.  It was on
a Friday afternoon, and with several rounds of beer downed,
Charlie Bill looked out the window and thought the world
had lost pigment.

Mr. Brock, the Everall man, was outside, bent over his
engine like a polar bear peeking into a cave.  The snow had
just about covered him.

The antifreeze inside Charlie Bill had settled and he felt
the patches of rose-red spreading on his cheeks.  His Celtic
origin caused him to be more friendly than normal on St. Pat's
Day and he zipped up his jacket, opened the door and pressed
toward the old man who was fumbling with his battery
cables.

"Need some help?" he called into the wind.

Mr. Brock turned his head, neck and shoulders toward
him in one motion and mumbled through his frozen lips.  He
was testy with cold, his eyelashes stiff with ice.

"Doubt you can do anything."

His words rolled out like snowballs.

Charlie Bill pointed toward his rattletrap Ford parked
next to the old man's brand-new Chevrolet Station Wagon.

"Jumper cables," he said.

He'd learned the hard way about missing an appointment
because of a dead battery.  Lost a sizable order for Rising Sun
from Harts Bakery.  For the most part, it pays to be helpful.  He
got the station wagon started and Mr. Brock offered him a job
selling Everalls.  As it turned out, the old man was nearing
retirement and looking for "a good man to know."  He trained

Charlie Bill, they split commission, then some years later Charlie Bill took over the territory. "You reap what you sow," but whenever he says this I wonder if it's true.

Because of the sudden snow storm, Charlie Bill busted around the South for some thirty-five years, the same as an old-time traveling medicine man, but instead of Wofford's Elixir or Abraham's Tonic, he sold the Everall. Sassy — that's what he calls my mother, though I never heard her called anything but Sarah — had wanted him to stick with Rising Sun and closer to home, but Charlie Bill could not ignore opportunity when it stared him in the face. He'd grown up wearing one of two pair of white socks. There was a big world out there with a lot of dead batteries in it.

Apparently this was the time when they became disenchanted with each other and split — *him* because he refused to be held down by a woman, *her* because she wasn't about to sit home while he roamed free, neither of them knowing that *I* was already a zygote.

Mr. Brock taught him the business with the patience of a mule driver. He shared the wisdom gotten from thirty years of road travel and spit out enough evangelism to save Charlie Bill and maybe four or five other traveling men from the wickedness ready and waiting in each motel and roadhouse.

Charlie Bill copied Mr. Brock like a shadow and from him learned "the four Ps"' — *Persistence, Pressure, Praise, and Presentation.* Charlie Bill kept his nose clean, his eyes on the road, and soon he drove a brand-new gray Ford station wagon loaded down with black Everalls, their red and white knobs lined up dress-right-dress, the hard work of selling made a lot easier by equipment that appeared able to do the job. Charlie Bill peddled battery chargers all over hell and half of Georgia — hardly ever came back home with one. A station wagon might not paint the same picture of prosperity as say, a Buick Sedan, but it held a whole damn squadron of Everalls.

Back then Charlie Bill was almost a "homing pigeon," thought he spent more time at Alex's than his rooming house, the same as he does now. He would leave the rented room at the beginning of each week, Sunday on his calendar, and travel straight through until Friday when he landed back at Alex's, which is where he is now. Where I am.

I'm on sabbatical from the university and have sat here a portion of each day for the last five weeks. Fate led me into the place — I stopped in for a beer after a day of research at the library.

Annie doesn't believe in accident — "You've been tip-toeing around him for years," she said. "Now that you know who he is, why not confront him and get it over with."

Mourning for a father I didn't know was a part of me, like body hair, and I wasn't about to shave it off so abruptly. Sadness, the bulk and weight of it, was what formed me, the essential ingredient of my wonder years.

At any rate, regulars in Alex's sidle up and, as part of the ritual, make some comment about the weather, never seeming to notice that it's the same in a bar day in and day out, and then introduce themselves. When the old man said "Charlie Bill Stone" and stuck his hand out, I said "Charles Wilson Moran," smiled broadly to keep my lips from trembling, and shook hands with him. If he knew the connection between us his face never showed it. In a menopausal funk, my mother had admitted the whole truth — that I was not the product of Wilson Moran, the grocer, but of Charlie Bill Stone, the wandering gypsy, the very thing that drove Wilson Moran to divorce her. He wasn't about to raise another man's wild oats.

"Priceless shit," was Annie's jab.

At Alex's they give everyone a nickname and since I teach history, they quickly dubbed me "Professor." The title seems somewhat ludicrous for a grown man attempting to climb a greased pole, but I say to myself, *Hold on there*.

Annie insists that my study of history supplants my real

need to find my own origins. Quite possible, I tell her.

"A knee grown from shallow roots of a cypress tree in a swamp glazed with green slime" is the way I like to put it. She moans, shakes her head and says I'm bound to slip in my own shit. Annie wouldn't like my saying it, but she talks much the same as my mother.

Marikoes stands Charlie Bill a round of beer and lays his quarters out on the table. Always the bus ride makes Charlie Bill tense and now he unwinds like a spool of thread. He puts two of Marikoes' quarters in the juke box and presses "It's All in the Game." He sips his beer and waits for Marikoes to make two more selections.

In this gathering of old men, the past flows into the present where it stands stagnant. I navigate Charlie Bill's past without a map, wondering what I will bump into.

"So what's happening out in the world, C.B.?" Marikoes most always begins their conversations this way.

"Armadillos," says Charlie Bill. "They've walked up from Texas. See 'um all over Mississippi now. I ran over one last time I was on the road."

*Ten years ago,* I'm thinking from my perch on the bar stool as I watch his faraway look, it's been ten years since you flattened the armadillo.

Marikoes nods and hunches his shoulders, sliding his finger down the list of songs.

Out there on the road, Charlie Bill saw many a peculiar sight; his list of wild animals caged out back of gas stations includes bears, snakes, deer, and llamas. But no armadillos. "People would stop and feed the animals scraps they wouldn't give an old dog," he says. "I'd always be tempted to open the cage and let the animals go."

From behind the bar Ernestine offers her opinion. "The owners had to make a buck somehow, now didn't they? Everybody does. Life's hard." The hard lines of Ernestine's face under the wiry tufts of gray hair show the truth of her statement.

I reach for the peanuts on the bar and imagine myself and Ernestine as animals running through the gate and into the woods. Set free by Charlie Bill.

Marikoes chooses "Alfie" and another tune that he calls a surprise.

"Alfie" makes me think of the marriage I stepped away from," says Charlie Bill, and I am listening hard now. He almost never mentions her, and rarely by name, but I wait for it to come. Instead he skips over to music, one of his favorite topics. "Times have changed, even here in Alex's. The music on the juke box used to be the best in the city. For all I know, it still is. Not much rock — and, for God sakes, not much of the fitful twanging from Nashville. Out on the road you can't get much else."

Marikoes' surprise tune sounds like the ocean. "New Wave," he says, and smiles at me in conspiracy that says that he's old in years but young at heart. He's hard pressed to keep up with his own wise-looking Greek face and I smile back as if he were one of my less gifted students who needs assurance.

Charlie Bill's short-term memory isn't much good. "What kind of music?"

"New Wave. It's like being in a dream, C.B."

Charlie Bill loads the quarters and punches "Have You Met Miss Jones?" and "Porgy" and "The Memphis Blues" and waits for the dream to end.

"They'll change all this to compact discs soon," I tell them. "You won't be able to buy records and tapes much longer."

"Everything changes," says Charlie Bill. "Up until 1977 you could only get burgers with lettuce, tomato, and mayo in here. Then *everybody*–but Lazarus — got into health."

Charlie Bill looks over at Ernestine behind the bar and says, "Give me a low fat cottage cheese, Ernestine. Hold the peach." He looks over at me, then at Marikoes across from him in the booth. "People try to give you fruit whether you have a tolerance for it or not."

"It's the fat content now," I interject from my stool. "Grams."

"Yeah. I heard that," he says. He looks at me and draws on the beer. "I guess I'd better keep account of all that, Professor."

Even if he could stretch out the curvature of his stoop, I am taller by several inches. Probably his mottled gray hair once looked sandy red the same as my own. Our eyes are blue. Forcing him into the present seems unacceptable and I wish I'd held back, fully understanding that more time must pass before I approach him with the news. I am a patient historian grubbing for my own history. Annie says, "Stop worrying over who fucked who when and get on with your life. He's an old worn-out wagon jobber. Low-life, about like your mother." Annie's a sharp saw. But it's not so bad when you expect it, *know* it's coming.

Lazarus sits rigidly at the far end of the bar as if rigor mortis had set in. He's the only one of the regulars who still smokes. He resents the imposed isolation and puffs earnestly to get even.

Ernestine gets the salad out of the cooler and takes off the plastic wrap. She cuts carrots in julienne strips and arranges them like a stack of firewood alongside the greens, then walks over and sets it in front of Charlie Bill. He munches the cucumbers, then quickly swallows a forkful of the cottage cheese, avoiding the taste.

"At least the furniture's still original," he says, looking at the barstools in my direction. "When they'd get rickety, Alex would just get out his auger and go at it. That's why they've lasted so long. Now the boy here does the fixing."

Alex, Jr., busily dries glasses and gives Charlie Bill the gift of his handsome smile. "Yeah. Yeah."

"Big Alex would be proud of you, kid," says Marikoes.

Kid repeats in my head. Alex, Jr. and I are about the same age. I imagine us as boys playing together at the foot of the shuffleboard table, sifting sand, throwing it in each other's eyes.

Alex's Bar and Grill, along with the Sports Club where Charlie Bill takes a steam, are solid establishments. "The best," he says. Other places just come and go. Above all, he is faithful to these places. I covet his sense of place and order a hamburger with lettuce, tomato, and mayo.

"Hold the peach," I hear myself say.

"Don't come with no peach," says Ernestine, setting me straight.

Lonnie the blind broom man taps his way through the door and into the bar, marking his steps. Charlie Bill cuts the lettuce with the side of his fork, but looks up when Lonnie comes alongside the booth. "Mr. Lonnie, you not speaking today?"

Lonnie stops and gets his bearing. "When's your birthday?"

"Born on April the second, nineteen and twenty-five," says Charlie Bill. "Just missed being a fool," and I wait to hear him say "No fool like an old fool," and he does.

Then Lonnie tells what day of the week Charlie Bill was born—Friday—a demonstration of his specialty. Charlie Bill buys a broom in appreciation and then gives it to Alex, Jr. Over the past five weeks, Charlie Bill has bought three brooms in what seems a kind of religious obligation. I envision bundles of brooms clustered in the corners of Charlie Bill's rented room, the affirmation of his faith, hope, and charity.

Suddenly I want a cake, one that is frosted with new-fallen snow. I want to tell Lonnie my own date of birth. July third, nineteen fifty-one! I want Charlie Bill to listen up—just be struck by it like the head of a blazing match, then quietly buy a broom and present it to me.

"So tell me about your heritage," I ask Marikoes just to get rid of the birthday blues. Jab a can full of holes and it sinks quickly. Marikoes starts up about the beauty and solemnity of the Greek Orthodox Church. His memories all seem to center on his childhood and I am certain he hasn't set foot in church for many years.

Lazarus coughs on his own smoke. He resents the talk of Christians. "They bring up the religion just to taunt me," he says to Ernestine.

"Quit sulking," she says. "I've never held you personally responsible."

Charlie Bill says that the closest he's gotten to a church in years is the summer night revivals he sat through out on the road for lack of something better to do.

"I never was visited by Jesus like Mr. Bock, mind you, but my ears got reamed out a time or two by the preachers." He says he can still hear Reverend Moon's thunder. "'And I say unto you, the man who fornicates with the Devil today will lie in a bed of hot coal tomorrow!'"

He tells this story to Marikoes who doesn't mention that he's heard it before. On that night, at the revival, Charlie Bill took a good look at the people around him who were listening to Moon, trailer people, dirt farmers and down-and-outers, just out lookin' for a comfortable place to sit for a while and air themselves.

The people squirmed in the heat, and inspired by the bellowing Reverend Moon, they poured fervor and one by one declared for Jesus.

Charlie Bill saved himself from religion by imagining that he was at a football game. When the lot of them stood up and hollered for Jesus, Charlie Bill got up and cheered for Lou Groza as if he'd just kicked a field goal.

Cubby Bear Callan walks through the door and slides into Charlie Bill's booth as easily as a hand into a glove. "Hi, Fossils," he says and then nods toward me. "Afternoon, Professor." Cubby looks as friendly as a little bright-eyed stuffed animal a child might carry around and I wave to him. When first I started this venture, I figured on quick satiation, then walk away forever. Now I feel as if I were looking down from the middle rung of a ladder, in danger of falling in with them and not able to get back up.

Charlie Bill looks faraway as if he's still out on the road. Alex, Jr. brings a bowl of redskins and sets it on the table, and Charlie Bill tells the story about the monument to the Boll Weevil in Enterprise, Alabama, and how the insect ruined the cotton crop and the farmers got rich planting peanuts instead.

Cubby steadily pops the redskins into his mouth. "C.B., you miss the gypsy life?"

"I've seen it all, don't want to see more," says Charlie Bill, moving the nuts away from Cubby. "Not even if they'd give my driver's license back. I stayed on the road way too long, but I had to save money for his college."

"College" tackles me hard and I struggle to get back up. She always told me *she'd* saved it, little by little, from the job at Kress's. Sometimes I wondered if she'd gotten the money from the men who came and went, and now I feel relief.

"I never was sure if he got any of it, mind you." Charlie Bill looks into his beer. "Later, I stopped sending. I figured if they were hard up, she'd let me know soon enough."

Lonnie works birthdays and brooms at the bar.

"Mathematical formula's not fair when it comes to you, baby boy!" says Lonnie to Alex, Jr., in a resonant voice that startles me each time I hear it, expecting instead a muffled sound to go along with the blurred eyes. "Your old man passed out Havana Coronas on that day. Nobody could forget!"

Ronnie Rosemary ambles through the back door and sits on a stool between me and Lazarus. Ronnie's an old mongoloid who has outlived almost every other one of his kind born in his generation, but even Ronnie seems to remember the day of Alex, Jr.'s birth. He mumbles and pretends to smoke an imaginary Havana Corona.

"The line's three and a half for the Bears . . . Giants game Saturday," says Cubby, tired of random conversation. He wants to land on sports and stay there. He pulls a pad and pencil from his shirt pocket, ready to take bets.

Charlie Bill recalls the fried gizzards they ate during the football games prior to the days of their good health. "Lou Groza was my main man back then," he says. "And old Alex was second. He did the frying." Young Alex now continues the tradition, except he does buffalo wings.

"If we could just put that mind of yours to better use, Mr. Lonnie," says Marikoes. "C'mon. Figure out the Giant's game Saturday."

"I don't bet on what I can't see," says Lonnie.

"What about the birthdays?" asks Charlie Bill.

"That's a sure thing. The writing's on the wall right in here." He knocks on his own head and smiles. His eyes roll all over hell and back.

Ronnie Rosemary spins himself around on the bar stool until he's dizzy, stares into the mirror for a few seconds, then closes his eyes and rests.

"He's daydreaming," says Charlie Bill. "Okay for him, but regular people have to fight against daydreams, especially out on the road. Daydreams turn the brain to grits. Out there I'd try to remember the name of every person I knew in a certain town. Mobile was hard — I knew fifty people there, but in burgs like Pontotoc, Lucedale, and Brownsville it was a snap. Sometimes I'd spell words backwards, or count cars with northern license plates. Anything to stay alert."

I pick up a handful of redskins and pop one into my mouth, and pass the bowl to Ronnie. I sit there and wonder what it would be like to walk around in a daze like Ronnie, eating nuts and daydreaming. No future. No past. Only the present.

"The one thing I daydreamed about was coming home and watching the Cleveland Browns on the TV. Always I'd buy peanuts in Enterprise and save some for the game. But when Lou came onto the field I'd put down the Schmidt and park the nuts."

"Schmidt," grumbles Lazarus. "*It* freezes before the *milk* does."

Charlie Bill looks at me. "Make sure Ronnie chews one nut at a time," and he continues his story. "The ball snaps, then Lou takes his strides, then whop — he kicks and the pigskin flies like an eagle." He raises his shoulders and his voice. Every one takes the cue and nods, even Lazarus. "Like watching hope," says Charlie Bill. He takes a long draw on the beer.

"Confidence," he says. "That was Lou. Whenever sales were down, I talked about Lou's toe. 'Steady as Lou's toe,' I'd say, or turn it around — 'his toe is as steady and reliable as the Everall.' Not exactly true, of course. Groza never missed, but the Everall was not entirely problem free — I figured that one out right off when Mr. Brock's battery went dead and with him cussing about having left it on charge all night."

Charlie Bill stiffens. "Mr. Brock was not all the time reliable either. One such time he got things mixed up and sent me off to a sales meeting. When I got to this building way out in the boonies, it was empty. Not one soul in there. That's when I split with Sassy. I got home earlier than she thought and caught her with this guy. Sometimes I think the building was an omen."

I imagine my mother entwined with her lover, not hearing the door creak when Charlie Bill comes into her lair and discovers them, then Charlie Bill as he runs to the car, guns the motor and roars out on the road, never looking back, while I, the zygote, lie helpless inside her as she disgraces us both.

Witness to her sin, I squirm to tell him. Sarah Moran, I say to myself and right then I know what Annie would say — You keep counsel with your own ass because you can't bear to admit your mother's a disgraceful bitch. Tell him. I embrace Annie's wisdom, my sweet and sour Annie, and right out loud say, "Sarah Moran."

Stunned, Charlie Bill's eyes widen and brim under a furrowed brow, and he suddenly begins a recitation of Lou Groza's statistics, starting with the late forties and steadily elevating his voice as he moves through the fifties, but stops abruptly in "nineteen and sixty-one" when Ronnie lights the cigar given to him by Lazarus. "Hey, Ronnie's not supposed to smoke."

"He's grown, ain't he? He deserves some pleasure."

Everyone glares at Lazarus. "Oh, all right," he says and takes back the cigar. He gives Ronnie an Evergreen Lifesaver instead.

Charlie Bill turns back to the subject of Groza. "No getting around it, of course. Lou had it all over guys like me. Never was much chance in Lou taking one in the groin. Big Bubbas were out there fronting for him." He looks toward me now and throws his voice in my direction. "In real life, nobody blocks for you. You take it in the gut. Keep hold of your confidence, stay with it and be prepared. That's the trick. It's like a black bird up there on a wire, minding his own business — you never know when the current might shock you. The hot seat. But you take it and go on."

Cubby Bear, Marikoes, and Lonnie all nod grimly behind the cloud of Lazarus's smoke. Ernestine quits wiping the counter and leans on the cash register. Looking at me, she takes a deep breath. "I think this pertains to you, Peaches. It don't have nothing to do with no Cleveland Browns."

Charlie Bill puts his cap back on, as if afraid what's on his mind might escape before he talks it out properly. "Before he retired, Lou was one of the oldest players in pro ball. He kept at it. If anything you should admire a man sticking to his life's work."

He looks at the ceiling and back down again at me.

"At one time I saw the numbers running up the odometer as money in the bank. I thought I'd marry and raise a couple of kids, buy a little house and pay for it body and soul the same as everybody else, but it didn't work out. Anyhow, nobody, I don't guess, ever gets done with the paying."

"That's true," I assure him, then lapse into silence. He's unrolling. I give him room for his scroll.

"The American dream was the reason for living out of a suitcase, eating artificial food and sleeping in the green and gold motel rooms at the Holiday Inn. And after things went bad, riding the highways flattened out the hard lumps and kept them from piling up again. I missed out on that house though," he said. "Most likely Sassy would have decorated the damn thing gold and olive green anyhow, same as the motel rooms. Every traveling man back then said the same thing. Green and gold. Even in the most expensive rooms. Even Lou Groza's, I bet. Every one of them the same."

Charlie Bill orders a large pitcher, then looks at Cubby.

"Might as well get the big one. You're gonna drink half of it anyhow. Beats me how a man not much bigger than a midget can hold more beer than a giant."

"As much as Lou Groza," says Marikoes. "As much as the whole damn Cleveland squad."

Cubby's little red face lights with pride.

"I guess the Browns gave up booze during the season," I suggest to Charlie Bill.

"Oh, yeah. Booze will kill you in the season."

I can wait no longer. Straddling a narrow chasm, I fall in. "Charlie Bill," I say to him. "Who's your next of kin?"

Through the bottom of the glass cross-cross lines over his face suggest infirmity. He moves his lips, groping for an answer.

"For Christ's sake," says Marikoes out of the side of his mouth. "His next of kin's Lou Groza!"

"Lou Groza, he's Italian," says Cubby. "C.B.'s not Italian."

"Thank God," says Lazarus.

I am the place-kicker, alone on the bench waiting for the

fourth down. Then Charlie Bill looks over at me and straightaway his face brightens. He motions Cubby to sit by Marikoes. And then it's my turn. I slide off of the stool and move toward his booth, stumbling clumsily, and take my seat beside him.

His elbow pokes in my ribs.

"He's Groza."

"Groza," I repeat, my wild son-of-a-gypsy heart pounding. The scattered sorrow mounds in place. Inside my head I hear Annie's words sawing to the heart of things and I hope she keeps counsel with herself. That she doesn't cut too deep.

\* \* \*

"Lou Groza" was originally published in the *Chattahoochee Review* and then reprinted in the author's short story collection, *Cold Eye* (Sartoris Literary Group). It is used with permission. Margaret Skinner is author of the novels *Old Jim Canaan* and *Molly Flanagan and the Holy Ghost* (both published by Algonquin Books) and the collection of short stories, *Cold Eye* (Sartoris Literary Group). A lifelong Memphian, she loves her city "warts and all." In addition to being a writer, she's an avid walker who grew up walking in Memphis Midtown near the Old Forest and Memphis Zoo and the banks along the Mississippi River. She has walked the 500-mile El Camino de Santiago in Spain and hiked the West Coast of Ireland.

**Jere Hoar**

# PREY DON'T TELL

## BY JERE HOAR

Charlie smells like musk perfume. He wears a green or maroon jacket with wide lapels, black pants with two-inch cuffs, black shoes with sponge soles, and an open-collar shirt that stands tall in back. The flat gold chain around his neck gets buried in gray hair that curls in the V of his collar. A college ring with a blue stone weights the third finger of his right hand. On the left hand is a band set with diamonds — not chips. He doesn't need knucks. He doesn't need a gun. Charlie is strong. "Just let some guy smart-mouth me," he says. "Just let them!"

I'm a keeper at the zoo, Jack Leonard by name, Jack L. by nickname. Smart guys say it like "jackal." I got a limp and I'm ugly. Now that Kally has left, I got Charlie for a friend. The lioness I'm in charge of don't like me at all. Or if she does, she likes me the way she likes any cripple' thing. She sees the hitch in my hip and says, *Uh-huh! Just you wait, cripple man. Just you wait!*

In Birmingham she clawed a keeper. They'd have put her down but she's so pretty we offered a trade. Got this fur on her neck like a lady's cape. Got a walk about her, and a talk about her. When I throw her meat chunks she chuckle down deep. *Thank you, cripple man*, she say.

Some evenings after work when Charlie ain't hurrying home to the good supper Kally cooked for him, or got a ball game to watch on his big TV, him and me sit outside the cat house and drink us some beer. "A twilight respite," Charlie calls it.

Charlie explains things to me. His eyes hide deep in his face, like in caves, and sparkle out little and bright. Charlie's maybe the smartest man I know, and the quickest. A man that crosses Charlie will have cause to wish he hadn't.

Drinking on the grounds is against all rules, but we carry our beer in a paper sack to show the night guards some respect. They make a wide circle around Charlie. One that joked about seeing Charlie drink beer got fired for sleeping on duty and carelessness with a firearm. None of the rest of them want to see the grounds boss drink beer.

Charlie and me don't call attention to ourselves. Just once we did. Charlie got the notion our oldest lion, Leo, needed some fresh meat. I took Leo on a chain to Monkey Island and let him look at them hanging in trees, screaming. I knew he wouldn't cross the moat to get him one. He's so old and spoiled he expects me to feed him.

When Leo came padding out of his cage, roaring loud enough to deafen a man, everything in the zoo screamed or barked or yowled or brayed. Leo showed his yellow snags and looked at Charlie. Charlie don't like to be in the thin center of a lion's eye  Leo made a little jump at him, but I got the chain and Leo ain't gonna do nothing. He ain't got it in him. But what does Charlie do? He runs.

I yell after Charlie, "Come back, Shane! Come back!"

Charlie comes back, draws himself up, and says, "Well, Jack L., I can retrieve my beer can, but I don't think I can retrieve my dignity."

I say, "How'd you move that fast, Charlie? I never saw a stout man run so fast."

"Let it alone."

I giggle.

"Okay, wise guy. What would you do if a lion came after you, and you didn't have a weapon?"

"I'd order it to its cage."

"Suppose that didn't work."

"I could run pretty fast if I had to."

Charlie says patiently, "No you couldn't. One of your legs is two inches shorter than the other."

I showed Charlie and Leo my Reeboks. "These are magic shoes. I been practicing."

"I can beat you in a fifty-meter dash, even with *this*." Charlie pats the roll hanging over his belt.

"You named that thing?"

Charlie's face gets hard like a rock. "Put that cat up. I'm going home and see what Kally fixed me for dinner."

"Stay awhile, Charlie. I got another six-pack."

"Get a life, why don't you?"

That night I ate two peanut butter sandwiches with sour pickles while I watched a nature program about wolves. When there is not a nature program on TV, I watch my tapes. I've bought all the predator tapes. I got a life. There's nothing better than living with predators, except maybe living with Kally.

"Jeez!" Charlie says the next time we meet for a drink. His lips tighten and he lifts his nose. "You smell like cat piss, man. You *bathe* in it?"

"No, I'm real careful, Charlie. I don't want to get any on me. Cat piss must hop on me from what cats have pissed on. It jumps like ticks do. That's what I figure."

"Where'd you acquire that idea?"

"I don't know. I just thought it up."

"Jeez! I don't know why I put up with you. You're nasty. You're inhuman."

"Kally didn't think I was," I say. My voice sounds whiny.

"Aw, kid, Kally felt *sorry* for you. You know how it is

when you get some poor crippled dog out of the pound, and you want to feed it and make it normal?"

"Kally liked me. I know she did."

"How could a woman stand a man that smells like cat piss?"

"You don't have to talk to me like that, Charlie. It's all right that you took Kally. I'm glad for her to live in your good house. I don't have nothing like that for her."

Charlie wipes the air with his hand and turns his face away.

"Here, have some beer. It's imported, Charlie. I was working late and didn't have time to wash like I should. I'll sit downwind."

Charlie reaches out a hand to feel the temperature of a bottle in the paper sack. Everything's all right then, because this is the Bass Pale Ale Charlie likes. He slips one out of the sack, fumbles in his coat pocket, and asks, as always, "You got the key?"

"Charlie, does Kally ever—you know, ax you about me? How I'm doing and all?"

"Naw." He gurgles the beer I've opened. "Kally don't *ax* me nothing. Do not say *ax* ever again to me."

"How is she?"

He shrugs.

"You used to brag on her. You used to tell me things she said."

Charlie rubs his jaw. He hums *Somewhere Over the Rainbow*. He gives me a sweet, sweet smile. "Will you shut up about Kally? Will you just *shut up?*"

"Charlie--" The whine that I don't want in my voice has come.

"Just one more thing. Does she *ask* about Duchess?"

"Naw."

"That sounds wrong. Are you sure?"

"She doesn't. I'm telling you."

I shake my head.

"Are you calling me a liar?"

"I don't know . . . Yeah, Charlie, I'm calling you a liar. You're *lying*, Charlie. You're *lying*."

I've doubled up my fists. I'm thinking about all the people I know who work big cats. We know cats better than people, and care about them every bit as much.

Charlie turns on the bench and pokes his red face toward mine. His yellowish eyes bulge. Every word sounds like a hammer tap. "She — ain't — ever — coming — back. Get Kally out of your stupid head."

"Why, Charlie, why?" I can't seem to stop my whine.

Charlie's words snap like whip cracks. " 'Cause I kicked her narrow ass out. She's gone. She got on the bus and left town. Took her brown suitcase and that hanging bag. We broke up. We split the blanket."

"Oh."

"So that's that."

"I guess."

"No more Kally. I don't have to listen to you carry on about Kally. Right?"

"I guess so." Something hurt in my chest. My throat felt tight and dry. My eyes wanted to run. I didn't have any taste for icy, imported beer. " — I guess that's right."

Charlie drank the six-pack of Bass alone.

For a while after I found out Kally was gone for good, nothing seemed to matter to me. I just went through the motions of being a keeper. Charlie tried to help.

"Jeez!" he'd say. "Stand up straight. You look like your damn back is broke. What do you care about that whore?"

"Kally wasn't a whore."

"Sure she was. Didn't I buy her off of you?"

"You never."

"Sure I bought her."

"She wouldn't do that." I was shaking my face back and

forth, hard. My cheeks and nose were swaying on my face bones. "I want you to take that back."

"Take it easy, kid. You're right, in a manner of speaking. A man couldn't buy her for twenty bucks, nor forty either."

"Not a hundred! She worked, hard work, in the cat house taking care of tigers."

Charlie smiled. "Okay, she worked in a cat house and wouldn't lay down for a hundred. But, she could be bought, Jack L. She went for the intangibles. Offer Kally intangibles and she'd open her legs." His voice rose to falsetto. "She'd say, 'Take me, take me.'"

"*Bull!* What's intangibles?"

"Stuff you can't even see. Good will . . . hot air. I gave her the words she wanted to hear . . . pictures made up out of air. I bought her for puffery. I said, 'Come live with me, Kally. I can't live without you.' That's what she wanted to hear. Coin of the realm with women." Charlie slapped his leg and grinned like we were equals.

"You told her you loved her. She told me you did."

Charlie wiped his hand through the air like a bear slapping bees. "Ah, you dope. If a man wants to get in a woman's pants the first thing he says is 'I love you.' Maybe he *does* love her while he's in heat. Or maybe he thinks he's in love because she's all he thinks about at first."

"You asked her to live with you," I argued. "You must have felt something."

"That's the peanut you give a monkey to do its trick. See, if a guy my age wants a young woman regular, it's what I have to pay. It's what I buy her with. *Now* do you get it?"

"You mean you lied? I get it, Charlie. I get it real good."

He wipes his hand through the air again, then brings it down and rubs his nose.

"Did I ever lie to you? I lie to people who hold their hands out asking for it, begging for it. I lie to the ones who say 'Give me the words I want to hear. I don't care whether they are true or not.'"

"It was wrong. It was wrong to bait Kally off her job and then throw her away when you was done with her."

Charlie sighs. "Nah, kid. It was *right*. That explains why I'm a supervisor and you shovel cat shit. I see the world as it is. You live in a dream world where the Blind Lady's scales tilt in favor of the dummies. That makes you as stupid as Kally."

What happened between Kally and Charlie I don't know, and may never know, but something did. Something soured Charlie. After he told me she was gone he hated female things. We sat on the bench at the lion habitat more than before. He had time for it. But Charlie stared at the Duchess with squinty, mean eyes.

"The zoo ought to get shut of that cat. She's a fugging menace," Charlie says. "You can't trust a female. Why do you come out here every night?"

"That beauty is very fussy. If I don't take care of her she will starve down to a moth-eat rug. Somebody got to do what's right for her."

"You're a natural fool," Charlie says. "Leo, he's steady and lazy. You can predict what a male will do. With Duchess you'll find you're a half-step slow."

I drink my beer and grin and belch.

"She hates me," he says bitterly.

"She loves me. Every time I go inside she takes the measure of my meatiest bones."

"You can't trust a bitch." Charlie has drunk many beers. His voice catches. "They'll step out on you."

Across the moat, in the habitat, Duchess walks back and forth, back and forth. She yellow-eyes us like we're impala on the Kalahari.

So, I had to know what happened to Kally. I took a vacation day. While Charlie was working I went to his house. It's a white frame house in a middle-class neighborhood.

Paint peels on it, and tall yellow grass stands in the yard. I went around back and looked in the kitchen window. Dirty dishes were piled on the table. Some stuff he'd thrown at the garbage can had missed it.

I popped the lock on the window with a short crowbar I'd carried inside my pants, along my upper thigh. Then I scrambled in.

The kitchen furniture was yellow Formica with rusty chrome legs. Leading off the kitchen was the den. It opened on a bedroom to the left and a bedroom to the right. Straight ahead was the living room. All the furniture was shiny oak. The couch was blue and puffy. The TV was a twenty-five inch Motorola. The unmade bed in the big bedroom had controls like the power console on a car. I smelled the pillows. They didn't smell like Kally. In a basket under the dresser in the bedroom was a six-month-old newspaper, seven ear swabs, and a cologne bottle with a label that said "Joop." I opened it and lifted the stopper. The Saturday night smell of it brought back Kally . . . her teasing and her playfulness and her smile. I pulled open the dresser drawer. The sight and smell made me close my eyes, weak in the knees. I picked up the boxes, the little brushes and lipsticks. I screwed the lipsticks in and out, thinking of them touching Kally's mouth. I read the labels of *liners* and *blushers* and *foundations* and things like that.

And I knew.

However Kally left, she hadn't expected to go. She would have taken her stuff. She always changed her face and clothes before going out in public. One minute she was a sweaty worker in a zoo you wouldn't notice. Forty minutes later she was a jingly, sweet-smelling, short-skirted flirt who caused men to smile and turn their heads.

Kally was crazy about Charlie. She didn't go away easy. He'd have had to beat her up something fierce. And she was strong. So when she left, if she left, her face would have been cut by Charlie's rings. She wouldn't have wanted me to see her, or anyone to see her, for a long time. Maybe ever. She wouldn't have looked like my princess.

So, I had to get even with Charlie, me with my little brain.

What I did was get some of the tranquilizer the vet uses when we work on the teeth of a bear. I figured out the weight of a bear and Charlie's weight, and doped his beer. We were sitting on the bench outside the cat house when I gave it to him. When he said, "You got a key?" I pretended the caps were tight on the bottles I opened. After he drank the second bottle, his chin fell to his chest.

I dragged him to the cat house, opened the door to the habitat, and dragged him toward the middle. After I cleaned up the drag marks I returned to Charlie, drank half a bottle of beer from my side of the carton, and poured the rest on Charlie's face.

He wakes up sputtering. "Where are we?" Charlie says in a dopey voice.

"The lion habitat. Smell something funky? I turned out Duchess."

Charlie sits up, propping his back with his hands. He looks two ways real fast. "You didn't"

"Yeah, I did."

"Where is she?"

"To your left. Maybe you can see the flash of her eyes. They look green in reflected light. She don't know what to do about us. She's looking at us and looking away. No need to think about the entrance. It's locked behind us."

"Put her back in the cage."

"This ain't Leo."

"Jeez, what are we going to do, Jack?"

"I don't know about you. I'm going to run for the moat. There's a gate there with a slide latch. I'm wearing my Reeboks."

"You can't outrun a lion, you damn fool! Nobody can."

"I don't have to outrun a lion. I just have to outrun you,

Charlie." I begin to laugh. "I just have to outrun dopey Charlie."

"Bastard!" he screams.

I stand up. Before I can move, he is on me, shoving me to the ground. Gravel cuts my elbows. He's stealing the advantage just like he stole everything I cared about. I grab his knees, but he kicks loose. I'm no match for Charlie's weight and strength.

He stands over me, then melts into the dark.

Duchess is coming. She's overcome doubt about what it means to have two humans in the lion habitat at night.

Charlie nears the moat. His form flickers across the beam of a streetlight. The moat is twenty feet deep and twenty feet wide with ten-foot fences close to each side.

Duchess's pads swish toward me. She's hungry . . . three days hungry. She smells the blood on my elbows.

If I look a little to one side at her in the dark, I can see her. Her eyes glow. Her yellow hide catches the light from the streetlamps and gives it back as a patch not quite black. The patch gets bigger. My spit thickens in my mouth. My breath whistles high in my nose. I lift my hands to ward her off. The odor of her hangs in the air. Then she passes me . . . is beyond me.

She has a genetic pattern to chase a thing that moves.

Then it happens. Maybe when he finds the escape gate is jammed. . . . Maybe when he smells her. Maybe when he hears the swish of her pads. Maybe when she hits him. Charlie screams. The scream breaks off clean like the snap of an icicle.

I don't need to see this scene on a TV screen.

When a cat is hungry she looks around at all the animals in the herd. Some stare back at her and say, *You can't catch me.* The lion thinks, *Which one can I catch?* A baby thing, or one that limps, or one that runs — that's what she can catch.

The first to run is the nervy animal that uses its energy

fast.

When a lioness catches prey, she bats it down like a kid does a Ping-Pong ball. The front paws hug it like she loves it. She nuzzles its neck for a choke hold. Her back feet fold up and rip down. Duchess's dewclaws are like cotton-bale hooks. But after she breaks Charlie's neck, Duchess doesn't know what to do with him. She drags him around the habitat, coughing and moaning.

I get the cage key out of my pocket, slip out the attendants' door, lock it, and pick up a fresh bottle of beer from my half of the carton. I drink half of it and pour the other half on my shirt. I reach up by the door and throw the emergency alarm switch that will ring in the headquarters building. The night watchman will see the light blink on the cat-house diagram on the map of the zoo and come running.

I limp into the dimly lit grounds yelling *Help!* I'm gonna sound drunk, but not too drunk, when I tell how Charlie wanted to play with Duchess like we did with Leo.

I'll have to stop them from shooting her, of course. But I'm sure that when I open her cage and call she'll come to the cripple man who brings the meat.

* * *

"Prey Don't Tell" by Jere Hoar was originally published in *Ellery Queen* magazine and is reprinted with permission of the author. Jere Hoar published thirty short stories, most in literary quarterlies, after retiring as Professor of Journalism at Ole Miss. He had studied and written in three fiction courses taught by noted writer Barry Hannah. His collection *Body Parts* was a *New York Times Book Review Notable Book* of 1998, the only university published fiction so honored that year. He received a gold medal for his story *The Snopes Who Saved Huckaby*, co-winner of the Pirate's Alley Faulkner Society's short story competition in New Orleans. Hoar has won the Deep South Writers Novel Competition, the Kansas City Arts Council Award, and his noir novel, *The Hit*, was reprinted by New American Library and re-published in France and Poland.

**Julie Smith in London at the River Thames**

# LOOT

## BY JULIE SMITH

Mathilde's in North Carolina with her husband when she hears about the hurricane — the one that's finally going to fulfill the prophecy about filling the bowl New Orleans is built in. Uh-huh, sure. She's been there a thousand times. She all but yawns.

*Aren't they all?* goes through her mind.

"A storm like no one's ever seen," the weather guy says. "a storm that will leave the city devastated ... a storm that..."

Blah blah and blah.

But finally, after ten more minutes of media hysteria, she catches on that this time it might be for real. Her first thought is for her home in the Garden District, the one that's been in Tony's family for three generations, but it's a fleeting one. She knows there's nothing she can do about that — if the storm takes it, so be it.

Her second thought is for her maid, Cherice Wardell, and Cherice's husband, Charles.

Mathilde and Cherice have been together for twenty-two years. They're like an old married couple. They've spent more time with each other than they have with their husbands. They've taken care of each other when one of them was ill. They've cooked for each other (though Cherice has cooked a

79

good deal more for Mathilde). They've shopped together, they've argued, they've shared more secrets than either of them would be comfortable with if they thought about it. They simply chat, the way women do, and things come out, some things that probably shouldn't. Cherice knows intimate facts about Mathilde's sex life, for instance, things she likes to do with Tony, that Mathilde would never tell her white friends.

So Mathilde knows the Wardells plenty well enough to know they aren't about to obey the evacuation order. They never leave when a storm's on the way. They have two big dogs and nowhere to take them. Except for their two children, one of whom is in school in Alabama, and the other in California, the rest of their family lives in New Orleans. So there are no nearby relatives to shelter them.

They either can't afford hotels or think they can't (though twice in the past Mathilde has offered to pay for their lodging if they'd only *go*). Only twice because only twice have Mathilde and Tony heeded the warnings themselves. In past years, before everyone worried so much about the disappearing wetlands and the weakened infrastructure, it was a point of honor for people in New Orleans to ride out hurricanes — to some people, with the storm of the century approaching, it still is.

But Mathilde is well aware that this is not the case with the Wardells. This is no challenge to them. They simply don't see the point of leaving. They prefer to play what Mathilde thinks of as Louisiana roulette. Having played it a few times herself, she knows all about it. The Wardells think the traffic will be terrible, that they'll be in the car for seventeen, eighteen hours and still not find a hotel because everything from here to kingdom come's going to be taken even if they could afford it.

"That storm's not gon' come," Cherice always says, "you know it never does. Why I'm gon' pack up these dogs and

Charles and go God knows where? You know Mississippi gives me a headache. And I ain't even gon' *mention* Texas."

To which Mathilde replies gravely, "This is your life you're gambling with, Cherice."

And Cherice says, "I think I'm just gon' pray."

But, as usual, Mathilde has to try, this time harder than usual because she's not there.

* * *

Cherice is not surprised to see Mathilde's North Carolina number on her caller ID. "Hey, Mathilde," she says. "How's the weather in Highlands?"

"Cherice, listen. This is the Big One. This time, I mean it, I swear to God, you could be…"

"Uh-huh. Gamblin' with my life and Charles's. Listen, if it's the Big One, I want to be here to see it. I wouldn't miss it for the world."

"Cherice, listen to me. I know I'm not going to convince you—you're the pig-headedest woman I've ever seen. Just promise me something. Go to my house. Take the dogs. Ride it out at my house."

"Take the dogs?"

Cherice can't believe what she's hearing. Mathilde never lets her bring the dogs over, won't let them inside her house. Hates dogs, has allergies, thinks they'll pee on her furniture. She loves Mathilde—you do after you've been with someone for twenty-two years—but Mathilde is a pain in the butt, and Cherice mentions this every chance she gets to everyone who'll listen. Mathilde is picky and spoiled and needy. She's good-hearted, sure, but she hates her precious routine disturbed.

Yet this same Mathilde Berteau has just told her to *promise* to take the dogs to her immaculate house. This so sobering Cherice can hardly think what to say. "Well, I *know* you're worried now."

She hears panic in Mathilde's voice. "Cherice. *Promise* me."

What can it hurt, she thinks? The bed in Mathilde's guest room is a lot more comfortable than hers and Charles's. Also, if the power goes out—and Cherice has no doubt that it will-- she'll have to go to Mathilde's the day after the storm anyhow, to clean out the refrigerator.

Mathilde is ahead of her. "Listen, Cherice, I *need* you to go. I need you to clean out the refrigerator when the power goes. Also, we have a gas stove and you don't. You can cook at my house. We still have those fish Tony caught a couple of weeks ago—they're going to go to waste if you're not there."

Cherice is humbled. Not about the fish offer—that's just like Mathilde, to offer something little when she wants something bigger. That's small potatoes. What gets to her is the refrigerator thing—if Mathilde tells her she needs her for something, she's bringing out the big guns.

Mathilde's a master manipulator, and Cherice has seen her pull this one a million times—but not usually on *her*. Mathilde does it when all else fails, and her instincts are damn good—it's a lot easier to turn down a favor than to refuse to grant one. Cherice knows her employer like she knows Charles—better, maybe—but she still feels the pull of Mathilde's flimsy ruse.

"I'll clean your refrigerator, baby," Cherice says carefully. "Don't you worry about a thing."

"Cherice, goddam it, I'm worried about *you!*"

And Cherice gives in. "I know you are, baby. And Charles and I appreciate it, we really do. Tell you what—we gon' do it. We gon' go over there. I promise." But she doesn't know if she can talk Charles into it.

He surprises her by agreeing readily as soon as she mentions the part about the dogs. "Why not?" he says. "We can sleep in Mathilde and Tony's big ol' bed and watch television till the power goes out. Drink a beer and have the dogs with us. Ain't like we have to drive to Mississippi or somethin'. And if the roof blows off, maybe we can save some of their stuff. That refrigerator ain't all she's got to worry about."

"We're *not* sleepin' in their bed, Charles. The damn guest room's like a palace, anyway — who you think you is?"

He laughs at her. "I know it, baby. Jus' tryin' to see how far I can push ya."

So that Sunday they pack two changes of clothes, plenty for two days, and put the mutts in their crates. The only other things they take are dog food and beer. They don't take food for themselves because there's plenty over at Mathilde's, which they have to eat or it'll go bad.

The first bands of the storm come late that night, and Charles does what he said he was going to — goes to bed with a beer and his dogs. But after he's asleep, Cherice watches the storm from the window of the second floor living room. The power doesn't go until early morning, and when the rain swirls, the lights glint on it. The wind howls like a hound. Big as it is, the house shakes.

Looking out, Cherice sees a building collapse, a little coffee shop across the street, and realizes how well built the Berteaus' house is. Her own is not. She prays that it will make it. But she knows she will be all right, and so will Charles and the dogs. She is not afraid because she is a Christian woman and she trusts that she will not be harmed.

But she does see the power of God in this. For the first time, she understands why people talk about being God-fearing instead of God-loving, something that's always puzzled her. You *better* have God on your side, she thinks. You just better.

She watches the transformers blow one by one, up and down the street, and goes to bed when the power goes out, finding her way by flashlight, wondering what she's going to wake up to.

The storm is still raging when she stirs, awakened by the smell of bacon. Charles has cooked breakfast, but he's nowhere to be found. She prowls the house, looking for him, and the dogs bark to tell her: Third floor.

"Cherice," he calls down. "Bring pots."

She knows what's happened: Leaks. The Berteaus must have lost some shingles.

So she and Charles work for the next few hours, putting pots out, pushing furniture from the path of the inrushing water, gathering up wet linens, trying to salvage and dry out papers and books, emptying the pots, replacing them. All morning the wind is dying, though. The thing is blowing through.

By two o'clock, it's a beautiful day. "Still a lot of work to do," Charles says, sighing. "But I better go home first, see how our house is. I'll come back and help you. We better sleep here again tonight."

Cherice knows that their house has probably lost its roof, that they might have much worse damage than the Berteaus', maybe even flooding. He's trying to spare her by offering to go alone.

"Let's make some phone calls first," she says.

They try to call neighbors who rode out the storm at home, but no one answers, probably having not remembered, like Cherice and Charles, to buy car chargers. Indeed they have only a little power left on their own cell phone, which Cherice uses to call Mathilde. The two women have the dodged-the-bullet talk that everyone in the dry neighborhoods has that day, the day before they find out the levees have breached.

Though they don't yet know about the levees, Cherice nonetheless feels a terrible foreboding about her house, acutely needs to see how badly it's damaged. She doesn't have much hope that the streets will be clear enough to drive, but she and Charles go out in the yard to clear broken limbs from the driveway anyhow. "Let's listen to the car radio, see if we can get a report," Cherice says, realizing they've been so preoccupied with saving the Berteaus' possessions, they've forgotten to do this.

She opens the car door, is about to enter, when she feels Charles tense beside her. "Cherice," he says.

She turns and sees what he sees: A gang of young men in hooded sweatshirts walking down the street, hands in their pockets. Looking for trouble.

Charles says, "You go on back in the house."

Cherice doesn't need to be told twice. She knows where Tony keeps his gun. She means to get it, but she's so worried about Charles she turns back to look, and sees that he's just standing by the car, hands in pockets, looking menacing. The young men pass by, but she goes for the gun anyway.

By the time she gets back, Charles is back inside, locking the door. "Damn looters," he says. "Goddam looters." And his face is so sad Cherice wants to hug him, but it's also so angry she knows better.

"Why they gotta go and be this way?" he says.

They listen to the Berteaus' little battery-powered radio and learn that there's looting all over the city, crime is out of control. "Ain't safe to go out," Charles says grimly. "Can't even get home to see about our property."

She knows he's sorry they came, that they didn't stay home where they belonged. "I'm gon' fix some lunch."

So they eat and they go out in the back yard, and clean it up the best they can, even try to get some of the debris out of the swimming pool, but this is a losing battle. After awhile they abandon the project, realizing that it's a beautiful day and they have their dogs and they're together. Even if their house is destroyed.

So they live in the moment. They try to forget the looting, though the sound of sirens is commonplace now. Instead of

Tony's fish, they barbecue some steaks that are quickly defrosting, and Cherice fixes some potato salad while the mayonnaise is still good. Because they got so little sleep the night before, and because there's no electricity, they go to bed early.

Sometime in the night, they awaken to a relentless thudding--no, a pounding on the Berteaus' door. "I'm goin'," Charles says grimly, and Cherice notices he tucks Tony's gun into the jeans he pulls on. She can't just stay here and wait to see what happens. She creeps down the stairs behind him.

"Yeah?" Charles says through the door.

"I'm the next door neighbor," a man says. "I've got Tony on the phone."

Charles opens the door and takes the man's cell phone. He listens for a while, every now and then saying, "Oh, shit." Or "Oh, God. No." Cherice pulls on his elbow, mouthing "What?" to him, terrified. But he turns away, ignoring her, still listening, taking in whatever it is. Finally, he says, "Okay. We'll leave first thing."

Still ignoring Cherice, he gives the phone back to the neighbor. "You know about all this?" he says. The man only nods, and Cherice sees that he's crying. Grown man, looks like an Uptown banker, white hair and everything, with tears running down his cheeks, biting his lip like a little kid.

She's frantic. She's grabbing at Charles, all but pinching him, desperately trying to get him to just finish up and tell her what's going on. Finally, he turns around, and she's never seen him look like this, like maybe one of their kids has died or something. He says only, "Oh, baby," and puts his arms around her. She feels his body buck, and realizes that he's crying too, that he can't hold it in any more, whatever it is. Has one of their kids died? she thinks.

Finally, he pulls himself together enough to tell her what's happened—that the city is flooded, their neighborhood is destroyed, some of their neighbors are probably dead, their own children thought *they* were dead until they finally got Tony and Mathilde.

Cherice cannot take this in. She tries, but she just can't. "Eighty per cent of the city is underwater?" she repeats over and over. "How can that be?"

They live in a little brick house in New Orleans East, a house they worked hard to buy, that's a stretch to maintain, but it's worth it. They have a home of their own, a little piece of something to call their own.

*But now we don't*, Cherice thinks. *It's probably gone. We don't have nothin'.*

But in the end, she can't go that way. She reasons that an entire neighborhood can't be destroyed, *something's* got to be left, and maybe her house is. She wants to go see for herself.

"Cherice, you gotta pay attention," Charles says. "Only way to go see it's to swim. Or get a boat maybe. There's people all over town on rooftops right now, waitin' to be rescued. There's still crazy lootin' out there. The mayor wants everybody out of town."

"That's what he said *before* the storm."

"He's sayin' it again. We goin' to Highlands tomorrow."

"*Highlands?*"

"Well, where else we gon' go? Mathilde and Tony got room for us, they say come, get our bearings, then we'll see. Besides, Mathilde wants us to bring her some things."

There it is again—Mathilde asking a favor to get them to leave. So that's how serious it is. Well, Cherice knew that, sort of. But it keeps surprising her, every time she thinks about it.

"How we gon' get out with all that lootin' goin' on?" she says. "Might even be snipers."

"Tony says the best way's the bridge. We can just go on over to the West Bank—we leavin' first thing in the morning. And I mean *first* thing—before anybody's up and lootin'. Let's try to get a few hours sleep."

Cherice knows this is impossible, but she agrees because

she wants to be close to Charles, to hold him, even if neither of them sleeps.

* * *

De La Russe is in the parking lot at the Tchoupitoulas Wal-Mart, thinking this whole thing is a clusterfuck of undreamt-of proportions, really wanting to break some heads (and not all of them belonging to looters) when Jack Stevens arrives in a district car. Sergeant Stevens is a big ol' redhead, always spewing the smart remarks, never taking a damn thing seriously, and today is no different.

"Hey, Del--think it's the end of the world or what?"

De La Russe is not in the mood for this kind of crap. "There's no goddam chain of command here, Jack. Couple of officers came in, said they got orders just to let the looters have at it, but who am I s'posed to believe? Can't get nobody on the radio, the phones, the goddam cell phones—" He pauses, throws his cell phone across the concrete parking lot. It lands with something more like a mousy skitter than a good solid thud.

He has quite a bit more to say on the subject, but Stevens interrupts. "What the hell you do that for?"

"Why I need the goddam thing? Nobody's gonna answer, nobody fuckin' cares where I am, nobody's where they're supposed to be and I can't get nothin' but a fuckin' busy anyhow. Nothing around here ... fucking ... *works*! Don't you ... fucking ... get it?"

"Del, my man, you seem a little stressed."

De la Russe actually raises his nightstick.

"Hey. Take it easy; put that down, okay. Ya friend Jack's here. We gon' get through this thing together. All right, man?"

For a moment, De la Russe actually feels better, as if he isn't alone in a world gone savage — looters busting into all the stores proclaiming them "open for business"; whole families going in and coming out loaded down with televisions and blasters and power tools (as if there's gonna be any power any time soon), right in front of half the police in the parish. Sure De la Russe could follow procedure, order them out of there, holler, "Freeze, asshole!" like a normal day, but which one of 'em's gonna listen? In the end, what's he gonna do, shoot the place up? It's not like he's getting any back-up from his brother officers and, as he's just told Stevens, it's not like he can get anybody on the goddam phone anyway. Or the radio. Or anyhow at all.

"Now, first thing we're gon' do is go in there and get you another phone." Stevens says.

De La Russe knows what he means, and he's not even shocked. What's going on here is nothing short of the breakdown of society, and he thinks he's going to have to roll with it. Something about having Stevens with him is kind of reassuring. He *is* a sergeant—not Del's sergeant, but still, if he heard right, a  sergeant in the New Orleans police department has just told him to go in Wal-Mart and loot himself a phone.

Just to be sure, he tries something out. "Loot one, you mean."

"Hell, no! We're gonna commandeer you one." And Stevens about kills himself laughing.

They hitch their trousers and push past several boiling little seas of people, seemingly working in groups, helping themselves to everything from baby food to fishing poles. Nobody even glances at their uniforms.

"Why are we bothering with the goddam phone?" De la Russe asks. "Damn things don't work anyhow."

"Yeah, you right," Stevens says. "But just in case." He turns to the busy knot of looters on the small appliances aisle and grabs himself one at random—a woman. Just shoves an arm around her, gets up under her chin, and bumps her up against his body. De La Russe sees her pupils dilate, her eyeballs about pop out of her head with fear. Stevens whispers something in her ear and she nods.

When he lets her go, she reaches in the pocket of her jeans and comes out with a cell phone, which she hands over meek as you please. Stevens hands it to De La Russe. "Now ya back in business." He swings his arms wide. "Anything else ya need?"

De la Russe feels sweat break out on his forehead. His scalp starts to prickle, and so do his toes. His heart speeds up a little. Weirdest part of all, he's actually having a sexual reaction; he's getting hard. Not all the way hard, just a little excited, like when he sees a woman he likes, maybe lights a cigarette for her, brushes her thigh, but that's all, no kiss or anything. A woman who isn't his wife but someone who's not supposed to get him excited. This is how he feels now, except with sweat and prickles. Because he's pretty sure this is not an idle question Stevens is asking. Thing about Stevens, there's rumors about him. About how he makes stuff disappear from the property room, shakes suspects down for drugs, little stuff that tells you a lot.

Thing about De la Russe, he's not above the same kind of thing. And he doesn't need rumors, he's been disciplined and everybody knows it. Yeah, he's been clean since then, but he's starting to feel this is something else again, this thing he's looking at. This thing that's nothing less than the breakdown of the social contract. It's just occurring to him that people are going to profit from this, and they're not just gonna be the Pampers-and-toothpaste thieves. He decides to get right down to it. "What are you getting at, Sergeant?"

"Hell, Del, it's the end of the world and you're callin' me sergeant—what's up with that shit?" But he knows perfectly well.

De La Russe smiles. "I was just wondering if I heard you right." He waits for an answer, not allowing the smile to fade.

Keeping his teeth bared.

"Remember that little eBay bi'ness you told me you and ya wife was runnin'? How she goes to garage sales and finds things she can sell to collectors? And then you photograph 'em and get 'em on up online? Y'all still doin' that?"

"Yeah. We still doin' that. Why?"

Stevens looks at him like he's nuts. "Why? Think about it, Del. You can sell just about anything on eBay." He pauses, does the wide open this-could-all-be-yours thing again. "And we got access to just about anything."

De La Russe is getting his drift. His mind's racing, going instantly to the problems and working on solutions. He shrugs. "Yeah? Where would we store it?"

"Glad you axed, bro'. Just happens I already hooked up with a lieutenant who's got a room at the Hyatt." The Hyatt has become the department's temporary headquarters. "He's got access to a couple other rooms we could use. And I don't mean hotel rooms. Storage rooms. Pretty big ones. We keep it there for now and when things get back to normal, somebody's garage, maybe."

De La Russe narrows his eyes. "What lieutenant?"

"Joe Dougald."

The patrolman almost does a double-take. "Joe Dougald? You're dreaming. Guy's a boy scout."

Stevens hoots. "Yeah? Ya think so? I been doin' deals with Joe for fifteen years. Trust me. We can trust him."

De La Russe isn't sure if he even trusts Stevens, much less Dougald, but what-the-hell, the regular rules just don't seem to apply now that the apocalypse, or whatever this is, has come crashing in on them. And he's got two kids in Catholic school, with college looming. *That*'s not going away.

He assesses the place. "Let's start with little stuff that's easy to carry. Ipods, video games, stuff like that. Electronics, small appliances. Hey, do they have jewelry here?" He gives a little snort. Wal-Mart jewelry isn't going to make them rich, even if it exists. "Watches, maybe?"

Stevens smiles, like he likes the way De la Russe is getting into this. "This ain't the only store in town, ya know. And stores ain't the only sources we got. You're from the Second District, right? People there got real nice taste."

De La Russe decides he's just fallen into a real sweet deal. Here they are right this minute, he and Stevens, policing Wal-Mart, and helping themselves while they're at it. He sees how he can patrol his own district, get credit for coming to work, arrest a few of the real looters--the street guys-- and help himself to whatever he wants while everybody's still out of town. How come he hadn't thought of it first?

It's early the next day when he sees the black couple — oh, excuse *him*, the two African-Americans — packing up their car in front of the biggest-ass goddam house in the Garden District, or so near it doesn't matter. What the hell are they thinking, there aren't any cops around here? He decides he's really going to enjoy this.

He parks his car and strolls up all casual, like he's just gonna talk to 'em. "How y'all?" Dicking with them.

They go rigid, though. They know from the get-go he's trouble, and it has to be because of their guilty little consciences. "What y'all doing?"

"Leavin'," the man says. "Gettin' out of town quick as we can. You want to see some ID? My wife works here and the owners are in North Carolina. So we rode out the storm here." He starts to put his hand in his pocket, maybe to get the ID, and that gives De La Russe an excuse to slam up him up against the car, like he thinks the guy's going to go for a weapon.

He pats the man down and sure enough, there is one. Doesn't *that* just sweeten this whole deal. Worth a lot to a couple guys he knows. "You got a permit for this?"

The guy doesn't answer, but his wife pipes up. "It's not ours. It belongs to Tony. My employer. When the looters came…"

De La Russe smiles. "…Ya thought it might be okay to steal ya boss's gun, huh? You know how pathetic that story sounds? Know who I think the looters are? Yeah. Yeah, I guess ya do. Let's see what else ya got here."

The woman says, "My boss, Mathilde…she asked me to bring…"

"Mrs. Berteau," the guy says. "My wife works for Mathilde Berteau."

"Right," says De La Russe. "Y'all get in the back seat for awhile."

"What about…?" the woman's already crying, knowing exactly what's in store for her. He grabs her by the elbow and rassles her into the car, shoving her good, just for the fun of it.

"What about what?"

"Nothin', I just…"

The guy's yelling now. "Listen, call the Berteaus. All you have to do is call them, godammit! Just call 'em and let 'em tell you."

* * *

"Like there was the least chance of that," Cherice says ten months later. The encounter had led to the misery and indignity of incarceration for three days and two nights, plus the humiliation of being accused of looting — almost the worst part, to her mind the hardest part to bear. But she has survived, she and Charles, to tell the story at a Fourth of July barbecue.

"Know why I was wastin' my breath?" Charles chimes in. "'Cause that peckerwood was enjoyin' himself. Wasn't about to ruin his own good time."

She and Charles are living in Harvey now, in a rental, not a FEMA trailer, thank God, until they decide what to do about their gutted house. Their families have all heard the story many times over, but they've made new friends here on the West Bank, people they haven't yet swapped Katrina yarns with. Right now they have the rapt attention of Wyvette

Johnson and her boy friend Brandin. Cherice didn't catch his last name.

Wyvette gets tears in her eyes. "Mmmm. Mmmm. What about those poor dogs?"

This annoys Cherice, because it's getting ahead of the way she usually tells it. But she says, "I nearly blurted out they were there at the last minute...before he took us away. But I thought they'd have a better chance if he didn't know about 'em. *Last* thing I wanted was to get my dogs stole by some redneck cop." Here she lets a sly smile play across her face. "Anyhow, I knew once Mathilde knew they was still in the house, that was gon' give her a extra reason to come get us out."

"Not that she needed it," Charles says. "She was happy as a pig in shit to hear we'd been dragged off to jail. I mean, not jail, more like a chain-link cage, and then the actual Big House. I ended up Angola, you believe that? The jail flooded, remember that? And then they turned the train station into a jail. Oh man, that was some Third World shit! Couldn't get a phone call for nothin', and like I say, they put you in a cage. But one thing-- it was the only damn thing in the city that whole week that worked halfway right. Kept you there a couple days, shipped you right out to Angola. But they got the women out of there just about right away. So Cherice was up at St. Gabriel—you know, where the women's prison is—in just about twenty-four hours flat. And after that, it wasn't no problem. 'Cause they actually had working phones there."

Wyvette was shaking her silky dreads. "I think I'm missin' somethin' here—did you say Mathilde was *happy* y'all were in jail?"

"Well not exactly," Cherice says. "She was *outraged*—specially since I'd been there for two days when they finally let me make the call. It's just that outrage is her favorite state of mind. See, who Mathilde is--I gotta give you her number; every black person in Louisiana oughta have it on speed dial--

who Mathilde is, she's the toughest civil rights lawyer in the state. That's why Charles made sure to say her name. But that white boy just said, 'right' like he didn't believe us. 'Course we knew for sure she was gon' hunt him down and fry his ass. Or die tryin'. But that didn't make it no better at the time. In the end, Mathilde made us famous, though. Knew she would."

"Yeah, but we couldn't of got on CNN if it hadn't been for you." Charles says, smiling at her. "Or in the New York *Times* neither."

Wyvette and Brandin are about bug-eyed. "See what happened," Charles says, "Cherice went on eBay and found Mathilde's mama's engagement ring, the main thing she wanted us to bring with us to Highlands. Those cops were so arrogant they just put it right up there. In front of God and everybody."

"But how did you know to do that?" Wyvette asks, and Cherice thinks it's a good question.

"I didn't," she says. "I just felt so bad for Mathilde I was tryin' anything and everywhere. Anyhow, once we found the ring, the cops set up a sting, busted the whole crime ring — there was three of' em. Found a whole garage full of stuff they hadn't sold yet."

Brandin shakes his head and waves his beer. "Lawless times. Lawless times we live in."

And Cherice laughs. "Well, guess what? We got to do a little lootin' of our own. You ever hear of Priscilla Smith-Fredericks? She's some big Hollywood producer. Came out and asked if she could buy our story for fifteen thousand dollars, you believe that? Gonna do a TV movie about what happened to us. I should feel bad about it, but those people got *way* more money than sense."

* * *

Right after the holiday, Marty Carrera of Mojo Mart Productions finds himself in a meeting with a young producer who has what sounds to him like a good idea. Priscilla Smith-Fredericks lays a hand on his wrist, which he doesn't much care for, but he tries not to cringe. "Marty," she says. "I *believe* in this story. This is an important story to tell — a story about corruption, about courage, about one woman's struggle for justice in an unjust world. But most of all, it's the story of two women, two women who've been together for twenty-two years, one the maid, the other the boss, about the love they have for each other, the way their lives are inextricably meshed. In a good way.

"I want to do this picture for *them* and... well.. for the whole state of Louisiana. You know what? That poor state's been screwed enough different ways it could write a sequel to the Kama Sutra. It's been screwed by FEMA, it's been screwed by the Corps of Engineers, it's been screwed by the administration, it's been screwed by its own crooked officials . . . *everybody's* picking carrion off its bones. And those poor Wardells! I want to do this for the Wardells. Those people have a house to rebuild. They need the money and they need the . . . well, the lift. The *vindication.*"

Marty Katz looks at the paperwork she's given him. She proposes to pay the Wardells a $15,000 flat fee, which seems low to him. Standard would be about $75,000, plus a percentage of the gross and maybe a $10,000 "technical consultant" fee. He shuffles pages, wondering if she's done what he suspects.

And yes, of course she has. She's inflated her own fee at the expense of the Wardells. She thinks she should get $100,000 as an associate producer, about twice what the job is worth. And not only that, she wants to award the technical consultant's fee to herself.

Marty is genuinely angry about this. She's roused his sympathy for the wrongfully accused couple, and even for the beleaguered state, and he thinks the Wardells' story — or more properly, Mathilde and Cherice's story-- would make a great movie for television.

However, he thinks Ms. Smith-Fredericks is vermin. "After looking at the figures," he says, "I think I can honestly say that you seem uniquely qualified to do a piece on looting."

But she doesn't catch his meaning. She's so full of herself, all she hears is what she wants to hear. She sticks out her hand to shake

*Well, so be it,* Marty thinks. *I tried to warn her.*

His production company doesn't need her. So what if she found the story and bought it to him?   He's not obligated to...well, he is, but...

Marty," she says, "we're going to be great together."

He shakes her hand absent-mindedly, already thinking of ways to cut her out of the deal.

* * *

"Loot" first appeared in *New Orleans Noir* (Akashic Books, 2007) and is reprinted with permission of the author. Julie Smith is author of twenty mysteries and a young adult novel, most of them set in New Orleans and starring one of her tough female detective heroes, a cop named Skip Langdon and a PI named Talba Wallis. She was editor of two *New Orleans Noir* short story anthologies. *New Orleans Mourning* won the Edgar Allan Poe Award for best novel. An ex-reporter for the *San Francisco Chronicle* and *New Orleans Times-Picayune,* Smith lives in New Orleans.

Corey Mesler

# Conjuration: A Fableau

## BY COREY MESLER

"A song is anything that can walk by itself."
Bob Dylan

In the days when magic was plentiful and sacred (rather than the vice versa we know today) there lived near Beale Street in Memphis a man of extraordinary powers name of Beaureguard Rawhead. He was, as a conjureman, quite remarkable, but he wanted to be something else. He wanted to be a songwriter.

He had seen W.C. Handy as a youth and he had been thunderstruck. Suddenly all his magic was as if nullified. He wanted to conjure something as powerful, as universal as "St. Louis Blues," or "Mister Crump."

And as he grew older, and his fame as a powerful magicman grew, the need to produce just one memorable song grew, too, until it was an authoritative obsession. So, when the bluesman, Tiny Red, came to see Beaureguard about some business, he saw the chance for a right proper tit for tat.

Tiny Red was from Arkansaw by way of New Orleans by way of the Orient, which is to say Tiny was a grabbag of musical inventiveness. You know him best for "Silver Dollar Pantleg Blues" and "A Frothing of Delight" and for inventing the phrase, "Your world." But, in his day, Tiny was as hot as they come, as big as Big Bill. In his tiny way, of course.

Tiny came to Memphis that fateful fall to scout up some talent for a travellin gig he was offered on the European continent. Most specifically he needed a second guitar and he heard tell of a Memphis bar rat name of Pete Holder played like the murmur of dreaming brooks. This was the word that he got.

He spent about a month on Beale scouting talent but he wasn't having any luck finding the elusive Mr. Holder. Some said they had just seen him, some said no he was in California. Some nights he was told he had just missed him. He's working at BingoBango, he was told, but no, when he got there he hadn't played there since last week.

But Tiny hadn't come to see Beaureguard Rawhead for no guitar player, no, naturally he came to see the conjureman for an affair of the heart. Seems Tiny had a major heartdeep crush on a dancer at one of the clubs, a woman with a rear like a Buick 6, comely like a pine bridge. Named Callie.

Tiny came, like so many before him, for a philter. He disbelieved in his own charm, in his personal ability to woo so fine a female, so he sought a charm outside of normal human makeup. A love potion.

Tiny knocked tentatively on Beauregard's tinplated door, anxious for thaumaturgy.

"Who?" Beau growled.

"Tiny Red Montgomery," Tiny swallowed. "From Arkansaw."

"Don't know ye," the answer.

"I need some help, sir."

"All God's children do."

"I was told you were the man to see bout this," Tiny said, a little bolder.

"Who said that?"

"Squiggly Robbins, for one. Bob Dobolina. Skincat Resin.

All told."

"You music man?" Beau asked with a twinkle.

"That's right."

"Bluesman."

"Yea. Yessir."

"You are welcome."

Tiny ducked entering the cramped quarters, dark as time. There was a jumble of material everywhere, tables piled with books and manuscripts, papers on top of an old upright piano, every surface obscured by knickknacks and gewgaws, objects seemingly floating in the air. One stooped, sidestepped, bent and shuffled to see the munificent wizard of Beale.

Who sat grinning in a burnished chair, a smile like a keyboard.

"Sit, sit," the old man gestured vaguely.

Tiny carefully pushed aside some papers and settled on an upturned crate.

The magicman fixed him with a milky eye.

"You know W.C. Handy?" he asked quickly.

Tiny hesitated. Know his music or know the man, he wondered. He had actually met the great man once in Montgomery, Alabama, in a dark club, shook his hand, even. This seemed like some kind of test.

"I play his supernal music in my act," he brought out, finally.

"Ahhh," Beau said. "I believe we can do some transacting."

The deal Beaureguard Rawhead laid out for the bluesman was simple but onerous. When he found out Tiny wanted a love potion (he coulda guessed, it was his main business) he allowed as to how he could grant him his every romantic wish in exchange for something a little less tangible. He wanted to be taught how to write a song.

Tiny rubbed his hand across his face, leaned back, leaned foreward again. He blew out a bit of sour wind.

"I dunno," he began.

"No deal then."

"Mr. Rawhead, writin songs. I dunno, it can't be taught."

"You learned."

"No sir, I was born writin songs."

"Naw," Beau said and he grinned like a warden.

Tiny knew he was gonna agree to this, he just wanted the disclaimers up front.

"I can try it, sir. I can sure try it."

"Thas all I'm asking, " Beauregard said, standing up.

Tiny rose too. The two men shook hands. They agreed to start that very evening.

That evening the sunset in Memphis was red like the blood of Abraham, the river sucking up that color like a lamia, like a mother dog. There was an eeriness in the air, a tone underneath the everyday, like a buzz in the distance, like cicadas from another world.

Tiny showed up on time, as the day was giving way to night. The old conjureman was eager to get started; he had cleared a space around his piano, like one might clear the ground to build a fire, or make a sacrifice.

Under his arm Tiny carried a sheaf of papers in a beatup folder, his songs. He spread those out on the piano keys and Beauregard glanced at them perfunctorily.

"Don' need these," he said.

Tiny stared at him a second.

"Mr. Rawhead, lemme get started. You need to learn the musical notation. This the language of the music, the alphabet. Can't build no song without this."

"Don't want to build no song. Wan to..." and he stopped, seemingly to change his tack. "Awright. I see. Teach me this," he said, tapping the sheets.

They spent most of that evening going over basic notes and melodies, Tiny using the out-of-tune piano to demonstrate the sound beneath the symbol.

It was 2 a.m. when he put his long arms above his head and

stretched himself with a crackling of bones.

"That's about it for tonight, I guess."

"Don't know how to write no song, yet," said the old man petulantly.

"Takes some time, sir."

"Awright, awright."

A week passed this way.  Small advances, stubborn setbacks.  The two men at loggerheads, butting them.

After two weeks the men were more cordial, whiskey between them, good talk.  They spoke of love, sex, the river.  A bond formed like electricity and the lessons took on a new compeerage.

And progress was made in the manufacture of a song.

Who woulda believed it?  Beau began to see the warp and woof of music, began to comprehend its sortilege, its special fluidity.  Music spoke to him in his dreams and waking he spoke back.  He began to hum around the house, tunes coming in like broken radio waves, indistinct at first, scattered. Gradually a cohesion commenced like his newfound fraternity with Tiny, some kind of coming together.

Secretly at first he began to cobble together a few lines, a phrase or two with accompanying melody.  A song was perceived through the dim, a strain appearing in the murk. Beaureguard in private seclusion was writing a song, unsure about revealing it to his master, the man who gave him music.

For his part Tiny suspected the old man was onto something.  A new lilt to his conversation emerged, a new lightness to his banter.  And in his muddy eyes blue stars danced sometimes, tiny shots like sparks off an anvil.  Magic commencing.

The party to celebrate the partnership of Tiny Red and his new guitar player (it was Andy Love due to the mysterious fact that Pete Holder never materialized) was held at the Club Bingo-Bango on a mild Friday night in October.  Word spread that there was to be an all-night jam and a number of the great and

103

near-great and never-to-be-great attended. At one sweat-retted point in the proceedings, there on the same modest stage sat in Mississippi Red, Alexander Jimspake, Styx Quetzlcoatl, Big Bill Broonzy, The Lonely Dog, Robert Jung, Jimmy the Snake, Ed Alexander, Pudding Puddinski the chanteuse, Roman Rebus, John Kills-Her (the Native American harp player), Squeaky Joint, Tuff Green, the Shawcross Brothers, Skeets Cameron and the Duchess herself. It was a callathump, a shivaree. A bombast. And it was the first time, historically speaking, that the word "bluesfest" had been used. It was coined that night. Write it down.

Long after midnight, the conversation a murmur of ghosts and drinking men, the air fuliginous, almost unremarked Beaureguard Rawhead slipped in through the back door. On the stage Styx and Peep-eye Harper were weaving a sleepy rondo, which sounded a little like "Back'em up Blues in D." Everyone was sorta half there and half woolgathering.

Beaureguard slid up to the stage and took a seat at the 88s and looked at them with a kind of wonder and amusement and the other two musicians hesitated and the crowd sort of hummed and burbled and there was a few seconds of dusty silence.

Beaureguard touched the first key with his left hand pointer and some other keys followed and before anyone could quite assemble their thoughts he started singing softly, almost to himself at first. The words were incomprehensible initially then took form and poured forth, Beaureguard finding a voice as thick as annihilation, as sinuous as ice. Tiny rose slowly from his seat in the middle of the dim and din and hung there like a suspended orb. It was a minor miracle. It was better than he thought possible. The conjureman had a voice, a reason to sing.

And it was on that night that the now standard number, "Saprophytic Blues" was born.

Beaureguard had a minor singing and songwriting career, nothing matching the magic of that firstborn number (though

The Latin Students had a minor hit with one of his songs, "They Bribe the Lazy Quadling" in the early fifties). His soul was at peace, however.

The other side of the bargain was, surprisingly, not as successfully achieved, even to making Beaureguard Rawhead cry out to his dark gods, "What good am I who cannot make the smallest world over?"

It wasn't that he gave Tiny Red a faulty philter, a no-motion potion. The elixir worked, oh yes.

Tiny took the small crystal bottle home with him and sprinkled it on his hairbrush as instructed. He lit the brush and it burned with a steady purple flame with a tiny red center like the back of a black widow as expected. But he never again saw Callie Pigeon, the woman he had so set his heart upon winning.

He went to the strip club to see her perform and was told she had disappeared. Poof, like a thought.

His heart ached and he knew an emptiness hitherto undiscovered, and he spent some lonely nights wandering Beale, in a trance-like funk.

He forgave the old conjureman, attaching no blame to the failure of the contract. He was sad but not bitter.

"I failed you, boy. I need to make it up to you," Beaureguard said, hangdogedly.

"It's okay, Beau. I'm okay."

"Man needs love, Tiny."

"It'll come."

"Let's go get us some Zombi Killers, drink ourselves outa the blues. What say?"

"I don' know, Beau. I don't feel right out on the street anymore. Something's wrong."

"What wrong?"

"Weirdness. Collywobbles. Somebody following me."

"Who do that?"

Tiny Red looked up at his friend. Tiny's eyes were deep sad, red-rimmed.

"Old woman. I look up. She everywhere I go. I dunno, she's okay, I guess. Kinda pretty. But, I don' need nobody following me, you follow?"

"Right."

The two men sat in stony silence for a few moments, the love between them like a cat. The air was tinny, faraway music somewhere.

"I get rid of that woman," Beaureguard spoke. "I make you a potion. By the way, Brother, I saw Pete Holder today."

\* \* \*

The story originally appeared in *Summerset Review* as well as in *Diddy-Wah-Diddy: A Beale Street Suite* (Ampersand Books, 2013). It is reprinted with permission of the author.

Corey Mesler has been published in numerous anthologies and journals, including *Poetry, Gargoyle,* and *Esquire/Narrative*. He is the author of nine novels, four short-story collections, and five poetry collections. With his wife, he runs Burke's, a 142-year-old bookstore in Memphis.

James L. Dickerson on the Natchez Trace

# THE SECOND COMING

## BY JAMES L. DICKERSON

A rectangle of golden sunlight shimmered on his desk, then tumbled over onto the carpet like spilled orange juice. He tilted back in his chair, hands nonchalantly cupped behind his head, looking alternately from the rectangle to a clock that peered from the shadows of the room, taunting the sunlight with measured metallic clicks that resonated like the firing pin of a revolver in search of a loaded cylinder.

Suddenly, there was a ripple in the golden rectangle, as it shuddered, blurred momentarily, then again settled into a shadowless coruscation that taunted him with its outlandish sense of place. He glanced at the window.

There was nothing there. It was unlikely anything had been there. Seventeen stories above the Toronto streets, there were few passersby. The ultramodern concrete cubicle in which he sat was only one among hundreds located in the towering Dominion Centre.

"Dr. Rubens," said a voice, breaking the tranquility. It was Dr. Aaron Rubens' nurse, Betty Trudeau, her face wedged between the door and the frame. She never knocked — and perhaps as a compromise to his imagined rights of privacy only allowed her head to venture into the room by the slightest of margins.

"Come in Betty."

With that, she strode across the room and dropped a file on his desk. "It's your last patient for the day," she said. "Mrs. Robbins." He tried to summon the resources to thank her, but all he could think about was how she had come between him and the golden rectangle.

Betty seemed to sense something because she continued to stand there, perhaps waiting for him to dismiss her. He looked into her eyes: orbs that were punched into a concinnous face that was fashionably framed between tightly coiled strands of black hair. The top two buttons of her uniform were fashionably unfastened. She had the hard hips of a twenty-two-year-old who knows where she wants to go in life. Women totally fascinate Aaron, which is probably why he does the kind of work that he does.

"Well," she said, whirling toward the door. "Guess I will get back to work."

With Betty gone, the room was a different place. The golden rectangle was still there, but it looked damaged in some vague way. As he watched, the rectangle slowly reshaped itself, scrunching up into a square. Soon it would be a golden square. In another hour or two it would be gone and the office would be dark. He wanted to watch longer, but he knew Mrs. Robbins was laid out on the examination table by now, her panties off and her feet up in the stirrups. He had been her obstetrician for several years and he knew how irritable she could get if kept too long in that vulnerable position.

Mrs. Robbins was the only thing that stood between him and his vacation. You would think he would have been waiting at the door for her to arrive, rubber gloves snapped into place, but things in a doctor's office are never that simple.

What if he found something wrong during the examination? What if he had to put her into the hospital and postpone his vacation? Shit happens.

Two weeks ago, one of his patients died. He delivered two beautiful babies. There were no problems during the pregnancy or delivery, everyone was healthy, and then two days after the mother went home from the hospital, she dropped dead. Fatty liver pregnancy, they call it. The liver fills up with toxins and eventually shuts down the heart like turning off a switch. There is no warning. She never knew what hit her. She thought she was perfectly happy. So did he. Those things happen. All pregnant women are at risk for the disease, but no doctor thinks it is going to happen to *his* patient. That's why he took his time going in to see Mrs. Robbins. Losing a patient is like losing your wife to a dentist and losing your job to a guy who wears sneakers, all on the same day.

Finally, when he could stall no longer, he went into the examination room. Mrs. Robbins smiled when he entered. She was a very attractive woman, thirty-two years of age and well groomed. She had two children before she started coming in to see him, and her twice-yearly examinations had been more or less routine.

"Be gentle with me," Mrs. Robbins admonished. She always said that, and who could blame her? He once tried explaining a pelvic examination to some of his male friends, but he didn't get very far, because they begged him to stop. Men don't like to hear about things like that. Mostly, his friends tease him about being an obstetrician. They think he became an obstetrician so that he could play doctor with beautiful women. That was part of it, to be sure, but after his first year any thoughts of that evaporated.

"Dr. Rubens, do you see any reason why I should not have additional children?"

"You're healthy—and you've got time yet. Have you been

having any problems?"

"I thought I felt a lump down there. Do you see anything?"

"Hmmmm," he said (why is it that patients like for doctors to make that purring sound when they are examined down there?) "There is a sight intumescence, but everything looks fine to me." He lifted the gown up past her hips so that he could examine her abdomen. Her muscle tone was superb. "You must exercise," he observed.

"Every day. When you hit thirty, every day counts."

Nurse Betty helped her with the top part of her gown, lowering it, so that it bunched up around her waist. "Have you had any fullness in your breasts?"

"I wish," she said gleefully.

"I see," he said, examining first one breast, then the other. Mrs. Robbins was a C cup, but dreamed of someday becoming a D cup. He discouraged her each visit from pursuing augmentation. As he pressed and probed, she continued to talk, her voice lifting at times as if she were about to become short of breath.

"Betty tells me you are going on vacation."

"Yes, we plan to leave in the morning."

Mrs. Robbins lowered her voice, intoning the phrase, "Hunka' hunka' burning love." She giggled immediately. "I'm sorry Dr. Rubens. I couldn't resist."

He hates it when people make fun of him, but the best reaction is always no reaction. At least that way, they usually shut up and move on to something else. "No problem," he said, broadcasting that unctuous smile they teach in medical school.

"I love it that my doctor is an Elvis freak," said Mrs. Robbins.

"Well, I don't know about freak — "

"Oh, I didn't mean it in a bad way."

After he concluded his examination, he stepped back

111

away from the table. "We're done here. You are in perfect health Mrs. Robbins."

"Oh, thank you doctor," she said.

"We'll see you in six months." As he passed out the door, he heard her say to Nurse Betty, "I always feel so much better when I see Dr. Rubens." They all say that.

When he returned to his office, the gold rectangle-turned-square was now little more than a faint crescent, hardly anything worth getting excited about. Nevertheless, he felt compelled to see it through to the very end. Perhaps that was the medical practitioner in him; despite his personal failings, he has a nurturing spirit. He approached the plate-glass window that overlooked the city. The sun was almost down. Soon the crescent would be gone and the sky would be black and the city would be ablaze with colored lights. He looked at his reflection in the window. He was nothing special to look at, he knew that. His hair was thinning. His nose was a little too large. And he had a mole just below his ear on the jaw line. Yet, despite those flaws, it is inescapable . . . he *does* bear a striking resemblance to Elvis Presley.

\* \* \*

"I need another strap."

Lisa stretched to pull down a corner of the tarp that covered the luggage rack atop the car. He tossed the strap to her. She had on cutoff jeans and a tube top, showing a little too much skin, he thought, but he was impressed by the tomboyish recklessness that showed in her coltish legs and muscle-hard midriff. Nearly eighteen, she was one of the most popular girls in her high school.

"Get it?" he asked.

"Almost." She yanked hard on the strap, then looped it over and secured it with an extra knot. She stepped back away from the car and brushed her dark hair back past her shoulder. "It's so hot," she said. "It must be eighty degrees. Will it be this hot in Mississippi?"

He laughed. "You kidding? This time of the year, it gets up to a hundred."

"No way," she said, searching his face for some hint of good humor.

"If it was good enough for Elvis, it's good enough for you." He grinned the way fathers have done since the dawn of time when closing off conversations with their daughters.

Lisa grimaced. "You said the 'E' word!"

About that time, there was a shout from the house. "You forgot this," said Priscilla, holding a large, flat box in her arms. Not just any box: The box that contained the jumpsuit, chains, and scarves.

"I didn't forget, honey. I was saving it for last so it wouldn't get damaged."

"Lisa, please come get this and take it to your father."

Lisa lowered her head, defeated, and trudged to the house. When she is doing something she does not want to do, she has this way of walking flatfooted, slinging one foot out in front of the other with the methodical motions of a climber moving up a rope.

"Smile, Lisa," said Priscilla. "You never know who's watching."

"Yeah, right," said Lisa, taking the box.

From the look on her face, you would think she was carrying a dead body. For some reason, she and Elvis never bonded. Aaron didn't really understand it, either. When she was an infant, he played Elvis records in her nursery. "Love Me Tender," "Old Shep," and "Teddy Bear." At her birthday parties he cranked up his best dance tunes — "All Shook Up," "Jailhouse Rock," and "Hound Dog." In the beginning, she seemed to be all right with it, but by the time she started to school, she had changed her mind. She never explained it. She just shut Elvis out of her life.

"The King's remains," she said, handing him the box.

One hour later, they were in the Volvo, headed for the Queensway. By mutual agreement they had imposed a moratorium on conversation until they were safely on Highway 401 West, too far away to return for anything which might have been left behind. Highway 401 would take them through London and on to Detroit. From there, they would drive due South to Knoxville, Tennessee, then over to Memphis.

The Toronto skyline followed behind the Volvo like a gigantic barge in tow; resisting the pull of the horizon, it seemed determined not to submit to the sameness of a straight line. From the rearview mirror, Aaron could see the imposing outline of the Dominion Centre.

Somewhere within that maze was his suite of offices — Dr. Aaron Ruben, M.D. said the plaque on the door. He liked to think of himself as a healer, at least on most days, but there are other days when he wondered just what the hell he was doing. He had delivered hundreds of babies and he had detected a few cases of cervical cancer, but he couldn't say that he actually healed all that many women. If you made a list of women who had been healed and a list of women who had died while in his care, it would be the latter list that would be the longest. That's not unusual for an obstetrician. That may be one reason why he turned to Elvis. In his lifetime, the King had healed the wounded and desperate hearts of millions — and he did it without asking anything in return, except for the price of a concert ticket or record album.

* * *

The sky was unusually bright, an intense blue, flawless but for a single grouping of cumulus clouds that seemed to have been caught in an act of flamboyance and paralyzed while tumbling away from the sun. The wind was slight, barely evident in the tops of the tallest trees. Scores of small farms swept past, emitting halos of pristine sharpness in the sun's blistering glare.

They crossed the International Bridge without slowing down, then came to a stop as they approached U. S. customs. There were ten to fifteen cars ahead of them. They turned off the ignition to wait. The smell of hot asphalt seeped into the car.

Suddenly, there was a commotion up ahead. They watched as border officials yanked a young man and his girlfriend from a van only six cars away. Struggling to get free, the man and woman cursed and pawed at the air, until, finally, the border officials forced the man to the pavement and shoved the girl out of sight on the other side of the van. After a while, they were whisked away, their wrists cuffed behind their backs.

Both the man and the woman were blond, with hair that dropped past their shoulders. They looked like actors. Aaron thought that maybe he had seen them on television giving the weather.

"What is that all about?" asked Lisa.

"I don't know," he answered. "They must be wanted for something. Maybe they are terrorists or something."

Lisa said snidely, "Or environmentalists."

Aaron drove up to where the border official pointed with his index finger.

"Where you headed?" he asked.

"Mississippi," he answered. "We're on holiday."

"How long do you plan to stay?"

"Two weeks at the most."

"Any plants or animals?" He peered over into the car.

"No, nothing like that."

"Have a safe trip," he said, and motioned them away.

* * *

Michigan was flat and unspectacular. Away from the big cities, it looked like any other rural area in North America. The highway was littered with rusting cars and backyards were filled with boats and aluminum sheds. Children, fat and listless, slouched on redwood picnic tables, eating the hearts out of watermelons.

In Indiana, it rained in torrents. Hastily erected road signs warned of flooding. Passing through the small towns, they saw people standing behind plate-glass windows, watching the rain. Not until they left Kentucky and entered Tennessee did the heat begin to affect them. It was not the gentle, sweet-scented caress they had expected; it was humid, stifling, a stubborn obstruction that flowed over them like the crosscurrents of a raging river. Lisa complained that she could not breathe. Priscilla sat quietly, wiping her brow with great wads of tissue. She smiled a tight little smile that made his foot slide down harder against the accelerator. She wondered aloud if it could possibly get any worse.

* * *

They arrived in Memphis at dusk. Aaron thought it was one of the strangest cities he had ever visited. Entering from the east, there is no skyline, only an endless array of strip malls, seedy hotels, and barbecue joints. The Interstate passes beneath a loop that circles the city and then penetrates several miles into the mid-town area. There it abruptly comes to a dead end. The highway was meant to carry travelers through the city into Arkansas, but was terminated by the state because of a scandal involving land purchases.

Aaron never understood why music writers always refer to Elvis as a country boy. Until he was successful, he only lived in two cities—Memphis and Tupelo. Memphis is the largest city in Tennessee and one of the largest in the South, and Tupelo is one of the ten largest cities in Mississippi, at

116

least when Elvis was growing up. To Aaron, there was never anything "country" about Elvis's music. It was gritty and raw, symbolic of the clash between urban and rural values.

In a way, that was probably what attracted him to the music; that sense of divergent cultures colliding with spectacular results; the feeling that it is what one becomes, not what one is, that ultimately concerns the universe; a sense of belonging to something larger than oneself. *I am only thinking this, you understand — I am not saying it aloud. I would never say it aloud, for obvious reasons. People have told me that my becoming an Elvis impersonator is symptomatic of deep psychological conflicts, especially since I am a physician; they say that as a man of science I should know better. But I say that is a load of psychobabble. Some of my Christian friends spend their weekends impersonating Jesus Christ. They wear flashy clothing and they stand on stages and make music. My Jewish friends, in their search for an alternate Messiah, spend their weekends doing much the same thing. If you really must know, I base my impersonation of Elvis Presley on the prophet Zechariah, who wrote: "And the Lord shall be seen over them, and his arrow shall go forth as the lightning: and the Lord God shall blow the trumpet, and shall go with whirlwinds of the south."*
*Sounds like rock 'n' roll to me.*

\* \* \*

They located the Commodore Hotel without much difficulty. It was downtown, facing the Mississippi River, where there is an actual skyline that, unfortunately, can be seen only from Arkansas. The Commodore is a plush, retro hotel with ornate fixtures, a throwback to the 1920s, when Memphis had more money than it knew what to do with.

The temperature in Memphis was about ten degrees warmer than it was in Nashville when they left, but that is typical for that time of the year. It was at least one hundred degrees, maybe even higher.

Priscilla and Lisa groaned and sighed all the way from the parking garage to the hotel, but the instant they entered the lobby they wilted into spasms of delight, for the temperature inside the hotel was at least thirty degrees cooler. It was like walking into a meat locker. As they went to the front desk, Lisa strayed over to a fountain that had lush green terrain in the center. She stared at the greenery, thinking she saw movement.

The desk clerk was no more than twenty, a lanky blonde with a sullen attitude. When Aaron gave her a Canadian credit card, she stared at it for the longest time. He said, "It's okay. It's good here." She gave him one of those "we'll see about that" looks and swiped it through the computer. A moment later she said, "Oh, it's been approved," as if it was the surprise of her life. It was the only time Aaron saw her smile.

As the bellboy gathered up their bags (he really was a boy, no more than fourteen), Lisa came running up to the front desk. She said, "Dad, you'll never guess what I just saw."

"What?"

"I don't know." Then to the desk clerk she asked, "What are those animals in the fountain?"

The desk clerk laughed, looking at Lisa with what appeared to be condescending compassion. "Those are armadillos," she explained. "The hotel keeps them there as sort of a mascot."

"Armadillos," Lisa mouthed to no one in particular.

On the way to their room, Aaron leaned over close to Priscilla and whispered, "I have a surprise for you." Priscilla looked at him with what could best be described as apocalyptic alarm. The elevator was creaky and jerky, emitting a low-pitched hum as they slowly went up. When the elevator door opened, Aaron had to help the bellboy with the bags, for he stumbled and almost tripped getting off the elevator. "Follow me," he said.

The carpet in the hallway was ancient, probably as old as the hotel. It had a musty odor to it that brought back memories of the older classrooms in medical school. The bellboy dropped the bags when they reached the door so that he could fish the key out of his pocket. Priscilla looked at him with apprehension, for on the door was not a number but rather a large lightning bolt. She knew what that meant.

When the door swung open, Aaron yelled out, "Surprise!"

He had reserved the Elvis Suite, the very rooms the King himself stayed in when he was unhappy with his mother or his father or his wife. Priscilla and Lisa walked into the room on tiptoes. The most prominent feature was an enormous circular bed, above which was an equally large mirror attached to the ceiling. Photographs of Elvis lined the walls. Across from the bed was a large-screen television and a kitchen sized refrigerator packed with soft drinks and ice cream.

"Where am I going to sleep?" asked Lisa.

"Yeah, where am I going to sleep?" asked Priscilla.

After the bellboy left, Aaron explained why he had reserved the Elvis Room. "It's gaudy, I know, but I wanted the energy of staying in a room where he slept. There is nothing remotely like this for Jesus or Gandhi or Mohammed. Just think how special you would feel, the energy you would absorb, if you could sleep in a bed you knew had been used by Jesus."

Priscilla looked at him the longest time, then excused herself to go into the bathroom to freshen up. Lisa looked around the room avoiding eye contact.

Aaron said, "How about it?"

She said, "Whatever."

* * *

As they were checking out of the Commodore Hotel, the

desk clerk sketched out a short cut to Tupelo, a road, she said was used all the time by Elvis. "You don't want to be on the main highway because of the trucks," she said. "They'll run right over you."

Lisa said goodbye to the armadillos, tossing bits of her breakfast roll to them. "Why don't we have them in Canada?" she asked. "They're cute in a creepy sort of way."

Priscilla took Aaron's hand as they went out the door. "I know I made fun of it at first, but I think I'm going to miss our Elvis room." Then she leaned over into his ear so that Lisa would not hear. "Especially that mirror."

Driving out of Memphis is not like driving into the city. That sounds obvious, but if you think about it, it's all being drawn versus the feeling of being expelled; leaving the city is like being propelled from a torpedo tube; you feel this powerful, invisible force pushing you along. The road out of Memphis is not an Interstate highway, rather it is a meandering, four-lane Mississippi road that is cluttered with businesses of dubious distinction and shotgun houses with satellite dishes, and mobile homes that appear to be closer to the road than good sense dictates.

"Help me watch for the turnoff," Aaron said. "It's a sign advertising catfish."

"Turn up the air-conditioner, please," begged Lisa. "I'm soaked. Look, you can see through this shirt."

Aaron most certainly did not look and Priscilla totally ignored the comment. Raising a teenager is easiest when it can be worked as a tag team. No one should raise a teenager alone. It should be against the law. When Lisa was born, there were complications and it was touch and go as to whether it would be a successful delivery. The doctor ended up using a vacuum pump to bring Lisa into this world; the result was a misshapen head that looked like an ice cream cone; Lisa was healthy and her head took on a normal shape within weeks, but the delivery resulted in a hysterectomy for Priscilla, which meant Lisa was their one and only contribution to the population of the planet. It was a tough break for Priscilla, because she wanted a large family, but she adjusted without it affecting their relationship.

\* \* \*

Aaron was not sure what to expect at the Elvis Festival, but it is probably safe to say that the reality of it transcended anything he could have conjured in his imagination. Police estimated that there were forty- to fifty thousand Elvis fans on hand, a number that more than doubled the population of Tupelo. They had a room with two double beds in it, but only because he had the foresight to make the reservations two years in advance.

The streets were packed with cars and campers, and local residents stood out in front of their homes with signs that promised parking for five dollars an hour. Stores that sold hardware supplies, videotapes, home-baked pies, and "high fashion shoes" advertised "Elvis specials." Once, as they stalled in traffic, an elderly woman in a white robe trudged past their car on the passenger side with a ten-foot cross slung over her shoulder. She looked at them and smiled, and then said to Priscilla, a glint in her eye, "That's all right, mama. I got you covered."

They had no problem with parking at the fairgrounds because Aaron had an entertainer's pass. They waved them right through. Scotty and D. J. were on stage performing when they arrived backstage. Aaron peered around the massive sound system that had speakers taller than he could reach and he saw a sea of faces out in the audience. He couldn't tell how many people were there. Twenty thousand? Thirty thousand? All he knew was that he had never seen so many people. They clapped, they swayed, they held their palms up in pious rapture.

On stage, Scotty and D. J. were like kids the way they mugged at the audience and spoke to each other through the music. Aaron tried to imagine what it must have been like to hear "Mystery Train" or "That's Alright, Mama" for the first time. Not performed for the first time — no, the way it sounded as it was being invented, the way it flowed out of the wellspring for the first time. That would have been really something.

Aaron, Priscilla and Lisa were there to greet them when they came off stage. Lisa and Priscilla thanked them again, as did Aaron, and Lisa told them how much she enjoyed their music. To her, they had taken on a romantic aura, larger than life, and that is something every young woman should experience. Aaron had never seen her look at anyone with so much admiration. Her life had been saved by the founders of rock 'n' roll: Aaron pitied the man who would have to win her heart.

Scotty asked Aaron when he went on stage and he told him about thirty minutes. Both men were dripping with sweat, so they excused themselves with a promise to "see ya' later." It is not often that a man can traverse that territory between the lowest point of his life to the highest in a twenty-four hour period, but that is exactly what was happening to Aaron. He had performed in and around Toronto plenty of times, but this was beyond anything he ever could have imagined.

On the way to his dressing room, Aaron ran into Amber and Sophie, two lesbian impersonators he had met in Memphis. Amber said she was having cramps, but she felt certain it was from the heat. Aaron took her pulse; it was elevated, but not dangerously so; he advised her to take it easy and not get over heated. She promised she would go slowly.

Aaron had worn the white, Elvis jumpsuit many times, but there was something special about putting it on this time.

Just as Jerusalem is important to Jews, Christians and Moslems, so is Tupelo, Mississippi important to those who subscribe to the gilded message of the King. This is where Elvis drew his first breath of life. People can laugh at that all they want, but it does not mitigate its essential truth.

The jumpsuit was a little wrinkled from being folded in the box for so long, but when he put on the wig and the extra-long eyelashes the imperfections of the suit disappeared. Aaron *was* Elvis Presley. Only allowed to perform one song, he chose "Jailhouse Rock." Considering what he had been through it seemed oddly appropriate.

Priscilla and Lisa were just off-stage when he arrived. He handed his tape to the soundman and waited to be introduced. Both Priscilla and Lisa had strange smiles, but when he asked them if anything was wrong, they both giggled and said no, only from Lisa it came out, "No way!"

When Aaron walked out on stage it was like nothing he had ever seen or felt. Instantly, he understood why performers become addicted to performing in outdoor venues; he could feel the love and adulation as it pressed in and enveloped him with a thousand arms. The applause was deafening when the song began—those trademark guitar chords slicing through the hot summer air with just a hint of danger and the drums mimicking a chain gang rhythm, sledgehammers pounding against rocks—but then the audience went into overdrive. They were so loud he could not even hear himself sing.

Thinking something must be wrong, he turned around and—to his surprise—saw Scotty on guitar and D. J. on drums, playing along with his tape. He was stunned. D. J. had performed with Elvis impersonators over the years, but Scotty had vowed never to do so. For him to be out on the stage with him was unbelievable. When he looked at Scotty, the guitarist smiled shyly and shouted, "Sing! Damnit, sing!"

He did. No one could have heard him, it was not possible because of the roar of the crowd, but that hardly mattered at this point. Aaron glanced at Priscilla and Lisa, both of whom were caught up in the excitement, jumping up and down with delight. For the first time since Aaron began working as an Elvis stylist he could see that Lisa was not ashamed of him. She pumped her fist at him like he was . . . well, Smash Mouth.

When the song ended, Scotty, D. J. and Aaron all walked off stage together, with the audience chanting, "More! More! More! More —." Aaron couldn't feel his feet touching the ground. He tingled all over from the vibrations of the crowd noise.

"Scotty," Aaron said, but he already knew what was coming next. Scotty said, "After what you went through to get here, I didn't have the heart not to help you out."

Just then Sophie ran up to him and grasped his arm.

"Please come!" she pleaded, her eyes frantic. "We need your help!"

They followed her backstage to the exit, then outside to a string of small buildings that were a permanent part of the fairground complex. She led them into a barn that, although empty of cattle or horses, had the unmistakable odor of equine habitation. Amber lay on her back, with her head on a cushion of gathered straw. When she saw Aaron, she smiled and held out her hand. He took it and knelt beside her. He could see that her water had broken, for it had pooled beneath her on the concrete floor.

"We've got to get you to a hospital," Aaron said. "Someone call for an ambulance."

"No," she said. "Not until the baby is born — please."

"I can't — "

Amber interrupted him with, "It's coming now — besides, you don't understand. It has to be you. My family is Orthodox. They finally came around to me being a lesbian, but if a Gentile delivers this baby, I'm dead." She smiled weakly and squeezed his hand.

"I'll examine you. But if it looks like there 'll be time to get you to a hospital for the delivery, then that's what I'll have to do. Understand?"

Amber looked at Sophie for guidance and then nodded at him.

"Lisa would you go round up an armful of towels — and find a clean blanket if you can," Aaron said. Then to Sophie and Scotty and D. J., Aaron said, "I need you to wait out in the hall, please."

Sophie leaned over and kissed Amber, then left with Scotty and D. J.

Aaron looked at Priscilla and gave her his most beseeching smile. "Are you up to helping me?"

"Just tell me what to do," she said, kneeling at his side.

Together they slipped Amber out of her Elvis costume, with her pleading every step of the way for them not to damage the sequins. Once Aaron could examine her, he quickly saw that she was correct in her assessment; the baby was on its way whether he called for an ambulance or not.

After that, things happened so fast there was no time to think, only to react; it is a place Aaron calls his zone of comfort, for it is as much an emotional state as anything else; the more frantic things become in the delivery room, the calmer he becomes (airline pilots experience the same phenomenon when things go wrong in the cockpit).

Within minutes, the baby was emerging. Amber began to panic, so he told her to sing. "Whole lotta shakin' going on, going on," she sang over and over again.

"Are you all right?" called out Sophie from the hallway.

"Whole lotta . . . yes . . . shakin' . . . yes!"

Lisa returned with a stack of towels and spread two of them out beneath Amber's hips and thighs. "Push," Aaron admonished her. "Push — and sing. Push — and sing."

"Shakin' going on . . . oh, God . . ."

The baby was moving quickly, but then stopped.

Something was blocking its way. Aaron called out, "Scotty — D. J. Do either of you have a pocket knife?"

"Yes," Scotty said.

"Open the blade and run it through the flame of a cigarette lighter. Make it fast!"

Less than a minute later, Scotty was at his side with the pocketknife. Aaron took the knife and quickly performed an episiotomy by making an incision in the vulva deep enough to allow the baby to exit. Then, as the baby moved forward, he realized he had an even bigger problem: the umbilical cord was wound about the baby's neck. He looked at Lisa and screamed, "Now — call the ambulance!" She was gone in an instant.

Every second counted now, for the baby's color was changing rapidly. Aaron reached into the canal, pulled the baby forward, then, once he had it all the way out, he juggled him from side to side and slipped the cord from his neck.

Like so many things in life, the margin between death and life often is measured in seconds. After a quick examination — all the vitals were strong and the external parts were where they needed to be — Aaron was certain the baby was healthy and he told the mother so. She wept, "Oh, God — let me see him, please."

Priscilla opened out a towel and held it in place while Aaron gently lowered the baby into her hands. As he tied off the cord, she handed the baby to Amber. By that time Sophie was in the stall with them and Scotty and D. J. were peering around the corner. The baby had thick hair, some of which looped down past his ears like sideburns.

Scotty and D. J. were stunned. The baby was the spitting image of Elvis. They stepped back into the hallway. "Did you see that?" asked D. J.

Scotty nodded.

"Looks exactly like him."

"Are you thinking what I'm thinking?" Scotty said.

"Damn right."

While they were out on the road in 1957, before Elvis's face became one of the most recognizable mugs in the country, Elvis saw a newspaper advertisement soliciting donors for a sperm bank. Elvis thought it would be a hoot to anonymously father some children, so he borrowed Scotty's driver's license (that was in the days before they attached photos to the licenses) and, using Scotty's name, went by a clinic to make a deposit into the bank.

D. J. said, "What cities did he do that in?"

"San Francisco and Dayton."

"Well, you know this girl didn't get pregnant the old fashioned way. She had to have help. How long can they keep that sperm, anyway?"

"As long as the refrigerator keeps it frozen."

D. J. said, "I'm going to ask her."

They rejoined them in the stall just in time to hear Amber ask if he minded if they named the baby after him. Aaron told them he would be honored. Sophie said, "We already had a name picked out, but this changes everything."

"I understand."

Amber nuzzled against the baby and purred, "Aaron, you've got a lot to live up to."

Everyone took turns praising the baby, commenting on what an excellent specimen he was; then when the conversation died down, D. J. asked what appeared to be an innocent question. "Where you ladies from?"

"Dayton, Ohio," said Amber.

D. J. winked at Scotty, who fought back a grin. "Nice city," he said. "We played there several times."

* * *

By the time they left Tupelo, Priscilla and Lisa both were

sorry to see it all end. They checked with Amber and Sophie before leaving, and they were just fine, as was little Aaron. They promised to stay in touch. Scotty and D. J. were magnificent. They, too, checked in on the baby and left gifts. They had dinner with them and they gave them directions for a short cut back to Nashville, by way of the Natchez Trace.

Lisa has two hugs in her arsenal: there is the fake, teenage hug, during which her hands dangle in the air, and then there is her real hug, during which she pulls the hugee in to her with both hands. She gave Scotty and D. J. her real hugs and promised to listen to all their old records. For an Elvis stylist, it doesn't get any better than that.

The drive to Nashville lasted more than three hours and gave them plenty of time to talk without the distractions of a busy interstate. Once they reached Nashville, it would be interstate madness all the way to Toronto.

Lisa was especially thoughtful. After a long stretch of desolate highway, she remarked, "Mom and Dad, something is bothering me."

"What's that?" asked Priscilla.

"Promise you won't get angry, but I can't figure out whether I am a Jew or a Christian. Why did you do this to me?"

"It could be worse."

"How's that—"

"Your mom and I could be gay, or one of us could be transsexual—and you would have to figure all that out and what it means for you."

Lisa laughed, then hated herself for laughing (*old people and their jokes*, she thought). "This is serious," she said. "Whatever I choose, it will hurt one of you."

"That's not true," said Priscilla. "We will love you no matter what."

"Promise?"

"Promise."

Aaron noticed a difference in both Priscilla and Lisa on this trip. He had no complaints before they left Toronto, but he found the new and improved versions very appealing. Lisa kept saying how proud she was of her father for delivering that baby and for the way he performed on stage, and her comments made him realize that while he had her love before they made the trip, he did not have her respect until now.

That is a sobering thought that all parents should spend a little time mulling over. Aaron's relationship with Priscilla changed on this trip as well, though he was at a loss to explain exactly why. It is one of those things that he could feel and see in her eyes, but not necessarily explain, not even to himself. Such is the power of Elvis.

* * *

"The Second Coming" by James L. Dickerson is published for the first time in *Mojo Rising* with permission of the author. Dickerson is a widely published author, novelist and journalist. He is publisher of Sartoris Literary Group. His many books include *Dixie's Dirty Secret*, *Memphis Going Down*, and *Scotty & Elvis* (co-authored with Scotty Moore). He lives just outside Jackson, Mississippi.

William Boyle / Photo by Katie Farrell Boyle

# INCIDENT AT THREE CORNERS

## BY WILLIAM BOYLE

Grissom presses Freddie's head against the dashboard of the Civic. "Forget about your old man," he says.

"You don't think God watches us?" Freddie says.

"You're gonna talk to me about God now?"

"I'm just saying, I should go be with my old man. God's watching."

"Your old man was the king of not showing up."

They're parked outside the Three Corners Pawn Shop on North Lamar in Oxford, right next Chuy's Place, a dive liquor store. The sky is tornado-weird. Doomy. An old guy's leaning against the front glass of Chuy's with a brown bag, watching them close. They're in Oxford for Nellie, but Nellie wasn't at her apartment and Freddie has no idea where else she could be, if not at the pawn shop with Russell. Freddie and Nellie's old man is sick at the hospital in Memphis.

"If Nellie's not in there or doesn't have the money, you're gonna score me the five large some other way," Grissom says, loosening up.

"I will," Freddie says.

"Damn right you will. What'd Nellie say when you talked to her?"

"Nothing."

"Now you've gotta hope Russell's not on his period."

"I know."

"I'll stay out here. You need me, come running."

Freddie nods. He gets out of the car and gives a little wave to the old drunk outside Chuy's. The guy's singing under his breath. Freddie can't hear what. He flattens his shirt and runs his hand along his jaw.

He goes into the pawn shop. It's all guitars and guns, TVs and toaster ovens. Russell's behind the counter, eating a plate lunch, looking sour. He's got a brand new axe out next to his food, sticker on the shaft. About eight times out of ten Russell's pissed at the world, but Freddie's hoping today isn't one of those times.

"Nellie around?" Freddie says.

"She's in Memphis with your old man. He just croaked."

"He's dead?"

"As shit."

"You're lying."

"Nope. While you were busy being Grissom's bitch, your old man choked on his soup." Russell smiles, flashing his raggedy yellow teeth.

Freddie falls to his knees. He feels like he can't breathe.

"You want a gun so you can kill yourself?" Russell says. "I'll give you a discount. Maybe Nellie'll have some peace if both you and your old man are out of the picture. Better yet, I'll let you use this axe Cubby just brought in. Can you kill yourself with an axe? Be worth a shot to try. Entertaining to see, anyhow. Lop off a leg for starters."

"I don't understand," Freddie says. "He's dead?"

"Nellie didn't even want to tell you because you're too emotional. I said, 'What're you gonna do, fake that he's still alive? For how fucking long?'"

Freddie throws up. The puke hits the floor and splatters across the front of his pants.

"Jesus, Freddie," Russell says. "Go in the bathroom. I don't want your mess in here."

Freddie gets up and wanders back out to Grissom in the Civic. He gets in the passenger seat, leaving the door open.

Grissom notices the puke. "What happened?"

"My old man's dead," Freddie says.

"Nellie wasn't in there?"

"Nellie's in Memphis."

"Well, that's fucking great."

"Didn't you hear me?"

"I heard you. Don't go romanticizing your old man, okay? Number one: you didn't expect him to live forever, right? Number two: he wasn't even good as far as pops go. Am I wrong? Tell me I'm wrong, Freddie."

"Let me have my grief."

"You can have your grief as much as you want. Long as you figure out a way to get me this five large."

"Fuck your money."

"What'd you say to me?" Grissom leans across the center console, nudging Freddie.

Freddie stares straight ahead at Three Corners. A red neon sign in the window says *P WN S P*, those three missing letters empty of light. One of Russell's sad handwritten notes is taped up next to it. Freddie can't make out what's on it, Russell's handwriting scratchy and tilted.

"All I've done for you, that's what you're gonna say to me?" Grissom says. "Your old man dying doesn't outweigh what you owe me."

"I don't owe you much," Freddie says.

"Get out of the car," Grissom says. "Now."

Freddie climbs out. He stands on the sidewalk in front of Three Corners. Grissom unlatches the trunk. He goes around and throws the lid open. He fiddles around a little in there. When he closes the lid, Freddie sees he's got an aluminum bat in his hands. His softball bat. He's used it to bust heads before.

Freddie was there when he clobbered Israel and Fernando. The old drunk disappears into Chuy's, the door clanging behind him.

"You should've just said something respectful," Freddie says to Grissom.

"I'm gonna beat your ass," Grissom says. "We came here for money, motherfucker. Don't you forget it. You lose sight of shit too easily. Always been your main problem. You agonize too much. Your old man's nothing, you're nothing, I'm nothing. What's a fact is we need that money. That's the only fact I know of right now. Hell, I'm not even sure your old man's dead. Who told you? Russell? You know he's a lying bag of shit."

Russell comes thumping out of Three Corners, the axe held across his chest. "You're a big tough guy with that bat, huh?" he says to Grissom.

"Go inside," Grissom says.

"How about you get in your piece of shit car and take off?" Russell says. "I got directions from Nellie to tend to Freddie."

"You heard from Nellie again?" Freddie says.

"I just texted with her. She wants me to bring you up there."

"You can bring him up there after I get my cash," Grissom says.

Freddie looks up at the sky. Gray gone green. Wind is kicking up. The world's a dull hum. He sees the weather as a manifestation of God's anger at him. He should've been there with his old man. No matter what. That's what blood is.

A blaring from behind Russell in the store. His storm radio going off.

"Hell's that?" Grissom says.

"Fuck a duck," Russell says, locking the front door. "We better go out in the shelter."

The shelter's back behind the pawn shop. A squat green

structure that seems to be secured to the ground with ropes and stakes. Russell leads the way, the axe held down along his leg. Inside the shelter, it's dark and carpeted and putrid-smelling. Bottled waters lined up against the back wall. Russell locks the door behind them. Grissom's still got his bat; he squats over near the waters. Freddie's fear has intensified. This tornado—if that's what's coming—it's for him, *because* of him.

"Fuck this weather bullshit," Grissom says.

"Man's gotta set aside his beefs when the weather goes rotten," Russell says.

A howling from outside. Wind like Freddie's never heard.

"When we get out of here," Grissom says, "I'm gonna have Freddie take that five large off of you, Russell, since Nellie's not around. Nellie thinks who she is. There's such a thing as having a code. My money's my money."

"You can try," Russell says.

"This is God doing this," Freddie says.

"What the fuck you on about, Freddie?" Russell says.

"I gotta take a piss, what happens?" Grissom says.

"You better hold it," Russell says.

"I'm serious."

"I'll chop your wang off before I let you piss on this carpet."

"There's no fucking tornado. You motherfuckers are paranoid. Seen a million skies like that. Most are bullshit."

"Yeah, well, excuse me if I don't gamble with my life based on your expertise."

Freddie weeps into his hands. "Christ, I'm scared," he says. "I'm paying. This is me paying."

"Freddie, you really think there's a God and that he gives a shit about you not being there to cry like a bitch at your old man's side?"

"That's why this is happening," Freddie says.

"Jesus Christ," Grissom says, standing. "Knock it off with

the God talk."

"Let the dumb fuck have his God talk," Russell says.

"God's brought this storm to me," Freddie says. "He's mad in his heart. That's how tornadoes get whipped up. I know that. I've been taught that."

"Who by?" Grissom says.

"A storm's just a storm, Freddie," Russell says. "Try to get your head screwed on right."

"A storm *is* just a storm," Grissom says. "But this ain't shit. This is the sky going wonky for a few minutes. It's gonna pass, and we'll all look like assholes for ducking into this stupid-ass box. You even hear anything anymore? I hear quiet."

Freddie starts praying. Prayers he learned from his mother. His mother's name was Gloria. She was eighteen when she had Nellie and nineteen when she had him and twenty when she left their old man. The old man was always trouble. Trouble was in Freddie's blood from his old man. That's one of the ways God matters, he figures. God sees that trouble and he works on you. It's like information travelling through wires. Freddie's old man was his responsibility because that trouble united them. They were both cracked windshields.

Nellie was with the old man when he died but she never had that same link to him; he was merely a burden to her. Freddie was a burden to Nellie too. His mother's prayers were the best prayers because she loved living. She loved living so much she died young. People who love living too much always seem to die young. She's in heaven. His mother's prayers are more hopeful than he'll ever be. He's ashamed now. He's sick. He deserves this storm. He won't go to heaven when he dies. He'll go where his old man is. They'll sit across from each other and that trouble will suck their faces together until they look like some kind of fucked up monster.

"Quit praying," Grissom says. "You're making me more

and more pissed."

"Let the man pray," Russell says.

"I thought you hate Freddie."

"I hate that Freddie's involved with you. That's what sunk him in my eyes."

"That so?"

"Yeah, that's so."

"I clobbered your ass with this bat, I bet you'd be singing a different tune."

"You can try."

Russell and Grissom continue to beat their chests. They get in each other's faces. The bat and axe crossed like swords between them.

Freddie stands and opens the door and walks outside. He's expecting to be swept away by a righteous tornado, but Grissom was on the mark. There's nothing. It was just a bullshit sky. They were being paranoid. There's no fucking God. Forget Memphis. Freddie goes into the shop and takes what's Grissom's and then he takes some extra for himself, including a piece that goes for three hundred bucks. He's ready for Russell to come charging in. He's ready to let *his* anger take over. He's lived enough of his life afraid.

\* \* \*

"Incident at Three Corners" by William Boyle is published for the first *in Mojo Rising* with permission of the author. Boyle is from Brooklyn, New York, and lives in Oxford, Mississippi. His novel *Gravesend* (Broken River Books, 2013) was recently translated into French and published by François Guérif as #1,000 in the Rivages/Noir collection. It was nominated for the Grand Prix de Littérature Policière. Boyle is also author of a book of short stories, *Death Don't Have No Mercy*.

**Sheree Renée Thomas**

# AUNT DISSY'S POLICY DREAM BOOK

## BY SHEREE RENEE THOMAS

"Want some candy?" Aunt Dissy asked when I was seven. Delighted, I thrust open my hand.

"Let me see it," she said. She grabbed my hand before I could hide it in my pocket, forced me to reveal the map that was the dark life lines of my palm. Aunt Dissy shook her head and laughed, her face like water, rippling between a smile and a frown. "See here? I told your mama when you were born."

The women in my family aged like trees. To Mama, Aunt Dissy was like a grandmama, more big mama than sister. Aunt Dissy was strong and clever, nimble-minded and sure. She pointed at a dark groove, a short river rolling across my palm. "Your love line all broken, your life line zagging, too," she said. She traced the pattern with the red tip of her nail."It's all writ right here," she said, her face resigned.

"Cassie, you ain't never going to be lucky in love, and you sho'll ain't going to be lucky in cards either. But don't worry." She leaned over, blowing peppermint and something stronger in my face. My bottom lip trembled, her bright jewelry banged against her chest. "You got the best luck of all, child, the best."

Luck? I was only in the first grade, and hope rose above my fear. Maybe if I raised my hand in class I would always know the right answer, I thought. Maybe if I didn't know, I could be invisible. Aunt Dissy stared at me, her eyes wide, knowing, bottomless mirrors. I wished I were invisible right then.

She dug her nail into the fat meat of my palm. I tried to focus my eyes on her thick silver ring, not the pain.

"You got the Sight." Her tongue held onto the "t," the word itself an incantation.

My face crumpled, my palm raw, exposed. For a moment, Aunt Dissy's eyes softened. She passed me one of her hard candies then stroked my palm with her rough, bejeweled hand, tugged at a loose plait curled around my ear. "If you don't understand right now, rest assured, babygirl. One of these nights you will find out in your sleep."

The red twisted wrapper fell from my hand. I stood petrified under the hard gaze of several generations of Aunt Dissys, hanging on the wall. Behind her heavy choker, I could see where there had been a deep gash in her throat. The scarred skin was raised and thick like a rope. Maybe the Dissys looked so sour because they were all cursed with the same "best" luck.

"Go on, play now," she said and frowned, as if she'd heard my thoughts, but I was frozen, didn't close my eyes for more than a few minutes for three whole days. Instead, I stared at the dark portraits that hung in heavy frames along the walls of every room. Imagined the navel names of the stern-faced women. Before, when I asked Mama about their names, she answered with one sharp word. "Dissy," she said and shrugged. So I fought off sleep making up a litany of names and stories about the Dissys' mysterious lives. And when the strain of wakefulness became too much, Mama found me passed out under the sink in the back bedroom, owl-eyed and babbling.

"What did you do to her?" she asked and carried me away. Aunt Dissy bit down on hard candy and grinned, the sound like crushed bones. I didn't find out until much later that Aunt Dissy poured whiskey in my tea, an old Dissy trick to force me to fall asleep. "The Sight's coming one way or the other, Faye." Mama unbuckled my overalls and put me to bed. "Even a mother's love can't change a child's fate."

Mama didn't speak to Aunt Dissy for six whole weeks. Didn't matter no way. Aunt Dissy had told me something else that scared me that first night. Peppermint couldn't mask the whiskey on her breath, nor those words she had whispered, as if they were a gift. "And with the Sight, you're going to live longer than the richest woman, deeper than the sweetest love." Coming from Aunt Dissy's lips, that didn't sound so good.

All day long Mama had tried to protect me, but when my eyes closed, I was on my own. And like all the others born before, not long after Aunt Dissy read my palm, the Sight came to me, just as she said, deep in my sleep.

That night I dreamed my room was alive. The walls, the doors, the ceiling pulsed and heaved as if they were flesh and breath. The room rattled like the tail of a snake. In the night, dark as the inside of an eyelid, I willed myself awake, refused to sleep for fear I would dream the dream again. But when I grew weary of fighting off sleep, I woke to a room that was collapsing all around me. Chips of paint floated down like peeling flakes of dry skin, decayed flesh. The walls hissed and screamed. I scratched the paint chips off of me, but they kept falling, dark and jeweled snowflakes.

My body felt dry and prickly as the brightly colored paint stuck to me, covering my skin. I screamed as the chips crept over my arms, my legs, my throat and face. Only my eyes remained. I could see the dream world caving in on me, but I could not escape. Something or someone was holding me, holding my breath. It forced my mouth open, forcing me to swallow. I tried to swing and fight but my arms felt heavy, weighed down by the rainbow tiles that covered my flesh. Neither asleep nor fully conscious, I fought between worlds. I couldn't stop seeing. A mosaic mummy, I scratched and clawed and screamed myself awake. The skin on my throat, my arms, even my belly were in tatters.

I cried for my mother but it was too late.

The night the Sight came to me, the night it ripped my flesh into cruel tattoos, Mama died. I never forgave the Sight for taking my mama away from me.

Aunt Dissy claimed it was a heart attack. "Yo' mama has always been weak." She covered the mirrors and dressed my wounds with raw honey, forced me to drink a bitter tea. As I swallowed the peppery spice, she refused to let me see her. She wrapped my tattered body in cloths and locked me in my room. But it didn't matter. I already knew the look of terror on Mama's face. As the Sight's fire crept over my body, burned through my shredded skin, I let the pain take over, allowing it to numb the pain of me being left behind.

I never got a chance to tell Mama what I saw in my dream. Every night I waited for her, whispered her name as I tried to fight sleep, but Mama never came. Only Aunt Dissy. And the others. When the oldest came to me, the very first Dissy, I recognized her as if she had always been there, hovering in my room. She floated in the air above me, the look in her eyes like two open wounds. Her body was covered in what I thought at first to be tattoos. But she was riven in cuts and runes. Even her blue-black face. The others gathered around her, rubbed ashes into the wounds. They covered her with a dark stained robe and gently braided her hair, dabbed petals from bright flowers on her unblinking eyes.

As they worked, I recognized them from the portraits that filled the walls in all the rooms of Mama's house. The woman with the regal black bun and the high, lacy white collar that covered her neck, the Dissy in the long skirts, with bright ribbons that hung down to her knees. The other dressed in sack cloth, her head covered in a handkerchief. Still another dressed in a cloche hat, sporting glossy marcel waves and a fur-trimmed coat, wrapped around her glorious figure. I saw another Dissy wearing what might have been a lab coat. She puzzled me. I couldn't tell if she was a scientist or held court in someone's kitchen. All of them Dissys, the infamous line of women in our family, women whose minds wandered in the realm of the spirits, returned with the answers in their dreams. And from what I could tell, their stern faces staring back at me from heavy frames along the mirrorless wall, none of them had been full of cheer. Ever.

So many Dissys. And still others came, from times I could not recognize. They showed me things I didn't understand, led me to places past fear. And if I refused to sleep, they would sing in the wind. They would whisper in the rain. They would linger in the shadows, the walls of my house shaking, humming, hissing until I slept, until I wove their signs into stories, some I whispered to Aunt Dissy, some I kept to myself. And when I refused them too long, the dark circles under my eyes like black half-moons, they would carve the dreams into my skin. Signs and symbols haunted me, a bloody warning in the light of day.

I wore long sleeves for years. The others teased me, said I was sanctified. I never kept up with fashion, for fear that one of the guidance counselors would think I was a cutter, for fear that CPS might take me away. I covered myself until women in ink were as common as night and day, and then I set the scars free.

For most, dreaming marks the end of labor, a time for rest, reflection. For me, it marks when my labors begin.

My dreams held the fates of people I had not met, their lives netted with my own. And no matter what I did years later to try to change my 'luck,' my fate, what Aunt Dissy said was turning out to be true. She'd lived longer than nature allows, while my own mama had died fairly young. Aunt Dissy had seen more dreams than any single mind should ever have. Her body held the story, just like mine. And at the rate I was going, it looked like I too would carry her burden, the weight of scars, the weight of years.

*Longer than the richest, deeper than the sweetest love,* she'd said.

But what's the point in living long if you're broke and lonely and all the dreams you hold are for everyone but you?

"Hey, Slim." I jerk my chin up in the obligatory greeting and watch Mrs. Medina's green beanpole of a grandson bebop his way down the street. He has gotten to the age where he thinks he's grown. He has three long hairs on his top lip he calls a mustache and some knobby strands on his chin he calls a beard. He believes he is a man now and can make a play for me or any woman he sees. If he sees even the hint of a curve, no matter how old that curve is, he's practicing on you. It's almost cute. He has grown tall and strong and brown over this Indian summer, but the baby, the boy straining underneath the skin of the man, is all up in his face.

I hear Katherine's little knock-kneed girls giggle as he struts by. His long arm waves as he gives them his back. Still wearing pigtails and bright bobos, they are too young to be *kee-keeing* in the manboy's face, but it's summer, such as it is, the ice cream man hasn't crawled by yet, and young hearts are for flirting, for loving, if nothing else. Or so I am told.

I stand in the shade of the fire escape, breathe in the scent of spices and my struggle herbs as the manboy disappears around a corner, down the brownstoned street. Aunt Dissy had the gift of green. Me, a different story. My rosemary looks dry, the peppermint and basil wilted, and the yarrow won't bloom. With my back to the kitchen, I can feel the spirits pulling the huge sky over me. The air feels heavy, humid, the weight of rain. Sheltered from the wind, my skin feels like ripe fruit about to burst. I haven't slept for nearly two days. A dry spell. Haven't had dream the first. Aunt Dissy's book sits on the kitchen table, atop its golden stand, its pages closed, judging me.

A lone black sock from the rough and tumblers upstairs just barely misses my head. That couple is always fighting. Everyone on the block already knows how that dream ends. I watch the sock sail down to the dirty street below, like a fuzzy feather, a sign or a warning. It falls in slow motion, a sign surely, but I don't know what it means. It's too early in the day and I can't tell which. The inside of my head itches. My eyes probably look like teabags. I'm afraid to look. In my mind I am two thousand miles away. My Sight is shaded up from the hot sun. Like a rainbow-tailed serpent, it won't budge until it's cool.

I close my eyes. Right now I don't want to see anything, don't want to hear, don't even want to feel. But I know he is standing outside the door before the bell rings.

"Come, sit down," I tell him and wave at the piano stool set up before my table. He sits as if the weight of his burdens has just sat down on the stool with him. His face and his thin shoulders worn down with worry, the remnants of his dreams linger in the wrinkles of a loose shirt that is too big for him. The man looks not much older than me, but I'm a Dissy — got more years than the stories in my skin can tell.

I don't offer him a drink or a cool glass of water, don't want him to get too comfortable here. The hard, backless stool is perfect, uncomfortable by design. When I had that old cushy armchair, fools asked me questions late into the night. The frightened and the lonely. The vengeful and the resigned. My head hurt, my eyes stung, and my mind was weary with their dreams. I couldn't get them out of that seat.

\* \* \*

You don't get what you want because you want it. The

waxy skin of my palm, the faded scars, remnants of a jagged river, was proof that not everything is meant for you. No, not love or riches, health or success. With Aunt Dissy's words in mind, I enjoyed the comforts of flesh, the mysteries of skin. Pleasure came easy because I never expected more. While others gnashed their teeth and wept at the comings and goings of lovers, my heart drifted above dry land, tumbled into dark caverns like water, slumbered in the shadows. Intimacy gave the vastness of my loneliness a sheltering look. His is the face of a man who might turn on you at any time. As if he was just born, already wary of the world.

"If I ask a question, will you tell a lie or answer me true?" he asks.

"Depends on the question."

He leans on my table—I hate when they do that—presses his palms into the indigo Adire cloth so hard, that I can see the dark lines on his knuckles, the veins running along the top of his hand to his wrist.

"Do you have the Sight or do you just need money?"

I stare into his black pool eyes, unblinking.

"'Cuz if it's the latter, I can pay you for your trouble and save us both the time."

He's got an accent I can't quite place. Something with a river in it, deep and Southern.

Can he see my discomfort or am I invisible? What is the right answer?

A lie or the truth?

He is not the first to sit in my chair, nor the first to ignore the signs, to will the impossible. Trying to change one's fate is a lifelong Sisyphean task, but to change another's is like trying to move a brick wall by hitting it with your fists. In the center of this knotted thought, your desire, is the belief that if you will it, change will be. Rest assured, the people who come to me have bloody fists. They sit in my chair, much like him, with disappointment or hope or both peering from the shadows beneath their eyes. And they expect me to move the wall for them, expect me to make a lie a truth.

I watch his hands, now cupped in his lap as if they hold a message. The remnants of his dream waft off him like invisible smoke, snaking through the air over to me. I don't want to be bothered but my utilities are due. Mama may have left me the house but she left plenty of bills. Utilities and property taxes so high, I had to break down and take on worrisome tenants. The sock puppets upstairs.

"Yes and yes," I say. He thrusts five folded bills in my open hand. I slip them in my trusted bank, adjust my bra strap, pat my breast.

Listen, telling lies is easier than reading, and reading is harder than telling the truth. It had been hard even with Aunt Dissy at my side. She greedily watched me as I slept, combed through every detail of my most mundane dream. It became more challenging without her, because I never thought I would be without her. Of all the Dissys who came to me, it's odd that Aunt Dissy never did. When she died, I waited for her those first weeks, but all I received from her defiant portrait was silence. And yet when she lived, I studied the ways and means, the art and the craft of reading dreams. And make no mistake, it is an art, the delicate task of mixing truth with half-truths, but she joined Mama and the line of Dissys before she could tell me all her secrets. Her death was a final sign of disapproval. The signs and symbols of the old policy dream book remained a mystery to me.

Truth be told, mistakes were made. After one mother came, her belly hanging low, her forehead riven with anxiety, that night I dreamed of a large sumptuous table. Luscious fruit, sweets, and bread were piled high around two bright brass candelabras with candles. I was so relieved to see the fresh fruit, the loaves of bread, I didn't notice that while one of the candles was bright, the other flickered in the dark, almost spent. I told the woman she had nothing to fear. Her son would be healthy, safe. So when she gave birth to twins, one who wailed in her arms, the other who shed no tears but was still warm, I counted her loss as my own. I grieved, for all I could see and for all I did not.

It was with her, that first mournful young mother, that I learned the power of nuance, the strength in ambiguity. Neither was for charlatans to hide, but for professionals to appreciate. Every square-toed soothsayer and two-boots traveler knew the universal sign for the conception of a boy, but I'd failed to see that the pair of candles in my dream meant that she would give birth to twins. A novice, I could see all the signs but I misread the symbols. Instead I'd spoken to the mother as if her child's fate was assured. A jackleg error is what Aunt Dissy would have said, a rookie rushing toward the finale instead of redreaming and working the scene.

Long after that mother buried her child, I wondered if he might have lived or if I could have better prepared her for the loss. But even if I had known, and told her that her son would die, she would have hated me still. Never to return.

Each day I woke with that mother's grief running down my face. But tears wouldn't help me. They never did. I had learned the hard way, the danger in misinterpreting a dream. It was almost as painful as refusing to see a dream at all, and I wanted nothing more than to be rid of Aunt Dissy's burden, my 'best luck.' I tried every drug and remedy I could find, lost myself in the forgetfulness of flesh, hoping something or someone would grant me the release of a dreamless sleep. But still they came, surrounded me. Dreaming awake, the Dissys watched from their gilded portraits, silent on the wall, the dream book waiting, as always, on its stand.

"A copious record of other's subconscious travels," one Dissy had written in her crowded, sloping pen of the late 19th century, but I could find nothing in Aunt Dissy's book that would offer me relief. With its smell of damp roots and weeds, its Old Testament-like list of names all handwritten by Dissys, reaching back generations, its hand drawn apocryphal images and inked sacred numbers, the dream book offered the key to others' fates, but for me it offered no answers at all. For all of its passages, handwritten and collaged, Aunt Dissy's dream book remained an enigma full of hidden, unwritten codes I struggled to decipher, blank spaces I filled with fear.

And it was clear that no Dissys dreamed of their own deaths, for where one scrawling hand ended, sometimes mid-sentence, another began.

\* \* \*

"What you see is not writ," he tells me, "not like in the Book of Life," he says. "You can be wrong, can't you? Sometimes it ain't all clear?"

I lie to him. After he tells me everything, about the unseen woman who haunts his dreams and makes him lose sight of his days, the faceless phantom, the haint that sabotages every attempt at love he makes. A lost love, perhaps, an old flame, an unforgettable ex? Most people who sat in that chair had more than a sore bottom. They came with stooped shoulders, bent from carrying the dead weight of the past. A relationship that would not be resurrected. Memories that should be put to rest and forgotten. But this was a different kind of hopeless, one unknown to me. I closed my eyes and rubbed my forehead, a finger at my temple, lying because despite the smoky tendrils of his dream, I couldn't see a single thing. The serpent slumbered, spent.

\* \* \*

Sky released rain. The day was leaving without me but this man was still here. I could feel the spirits around me, hear them pounding the streets outside my window, but I couldn't get this man out of my chair. His sadness was a long, unbroken note slowly descending into madness.

Anything else I could say would sound reedy, hollow to his ear. I could tell from his face. He was one of those hard-headed, fingers in your split side souls. I would have to show him. This is where the cards become more than props.

I pull out the pouch. Its worn purple velvet is smooth in my hand, the royal yellow stitching now only reads "CROW."

"You're going to read Tarot?" he asks, incredulous. He glares at the discarded crystals and the bowl of red brick dust, both silent failures atop the lacy table. I have already tried everything. He is not impressed. "Been there, done that," he says. His old genteel Bojangles act discarded, too. "Death card comes up every time, don't mean shit."

He's right. Skeletons and bones, black knights on white horses. Mine is a great dying baobab, the tree of life, cut down with a bone ax. A Dissy from the 1920s called the weapon the Bonecarver. She even sketched the ax, a drawing I used to make my tarot. I stroke the purple velvet pouch, unloosening the yellow cord even as he protests.

Death, the thirteenth trump, a major arcana, represents significant change. Transformation, endings, and new beginnings. I shuffle and reshuffle the deck, stall for time, hoping for some kind of inner vision. Nothing comes through, not even a dirty sock tossed out a window.

He shakes his head. He doesn't want to hear any of this.

"You got to close one door to open another," I say, stalling.

"Whatever. Just tell me what you see."

I'm tired. I drop the cards. He is closed to me. Just like Aunt Dissy. Distrustful and secretive, she never let me see her dreams. "That's the problem. I can't," I say. I can't look him in the eye. "I, I have to sleep with you."

His brow shoots up, his sad mouth almost turned to a half smile. "You what?"

"No." The words aren't coming out right. I feel like I'm already sleepwalking in a dream. "I mean I am going to have to sleep, to see…" my voice trails off. No sane way to explain it.

He studies me coolly. "You're telling me you're trying to go to sleep in the middle of the job? Go ahead then. I'll be here when you wake."

That's not what I expected. I study his face again. Now it's my turn to protest, but he stops me, bloody fists still hitting that wall. "I don't know if I can explain it, but Mrs. Bannister —"

"Cassie. Mrs. Bannister was my aunt."

"Cassie," he said it as if it pained him. "It's really important that I get some closure here. I can't —" He stares at the backs of his hands. "I can't keep living like this. I was engaged. We, we could have been happy but I — I need to know who this other woman is, what she is. I don't care about being with her or not. I just want this, not knowing to be over. So I can make a decision."

Something in his words tug at me. He is ripping up the whole damn script. Most people sitting in that chair wanted that other relationship no matter what. They wanted assurance. A sign that what they hoped for would come true. But this man didn't even know who he was pining for. This one just wanted closure. He wanted to sleep at night — but don't we all? Wanted to know and to walk away — or so he claimed. I wasn't yet sure if he was the letting go kind or, like my upstairs tenants, the kind with the stranglehold.

He told me how he first encountered her, in some old childhood nightmare of a dream that clearly scarred him for life. Typical guilty conscious mess. But as he spoke, suddenly the silvery threads of his dreams circled around his throat, coiled in the air, weaving and unweaving themselves like silk webs, shrinking then growing longer as they covered me, a gossamer cape until my eyes closed. A sea of blue green sapphires opened up and I stepped inside to see.

In this dream the ground is chill, wet underfoot, the air

laced with sweet perfumes. Honeysuckle and moon musk sting my eyes, sibilant leaves prick my scalp from up above. I walk to an aged willow tree, groaning its complaints to a brook. Aunt Dissy taught me the language of trees. Sometimes they offer you real clues. Most of the time they're just bitching. This one complains about a bruise, a burden too heavy, a man named Iudas. Old dirt he needs to get over. I tune out the trees and adjust until my eyes grow accustomed to the darkness. I know the woman is there but cannot see her face.

She is hiding from me. I am not in the mood. "Look, lady," I call out, trying to keep up with her. "I'm not trying to get in your business or nothing, it's just that..." *Wait. Is this woman running from me? Oh, hell no!* As she flees, she's stripping, dropping whole swaths of cloth, brightly colored, glittering in the night. By now she is probably buck naked and there is no way I am following her into those woods. She is going to have to Hansel-and-Gretel on her own.

Night is never quite as dark as you think. There is always some starshine, some moonbeam, firefly glow. But not here. Wherever the woman disappeared to is like a black hole floating in the middle of the night. The backs of my eyes are itching, my eyelids and elbows twitching like a needle scratching on a record. I waver in the narrow band of zodiacal light, the faint luminosity of the horizon, the memory of a day that will not come again, the promise of a new one that has yet to begin.

Ravens circle my head—a really fucked up sign—I swing at them and moonwalk my way back out of his dream. Like the others, he knows what he wants but he has no idea what he needs. He is asking me to peer into the darkness, asking me to see past what was to what could be. I tell him there is no harder work than imagining a future.

"Hold the deck," I command, eyes still closed. Time for some theater. He hesitates. "Don't worry," I say, opening my eyes slowly. "They won't hurt you." *Bless his heart.* He thinks

I'm talking about the cards. He grips them, his sad mouth now a defiant frown. I take the cards from him, still warm from his touch, and spread them out in a fan. "Choose three." He studies the backs of the cards, his eyes narrowing at the design, a raven caught in the thick limbs of the blossoming world tree.

As I watch him decide, I wonder if I could love someone with the same unforgiving force that pushed forests from the deep ground. People think because they forget their dreams, that they are gone. They are not. The body holds them, the way rich soil holds water. Dreams are hidden somewhere deep in the bones, and flesh, and skin. The residue of his recurring dream hovered around him like a sweet musk, like sweat. With its scent I could feel the Sight stir inside of me, uncoiling again from the back of my brain like a waking snake.

He watches my face, unaware that I am still dreaming even as he sneers at me. He tries to look indifferent, but his eyes are now as sad as his mouth.

I try to recall the woman's shimmering steps. In the dream her path is the same. Down a road she doesn't want to travel, with branches for legs and twigs for hands. Raven's feathers pour from her mouth. A filthy starless sky of rain and blackbirds pierce the clouds, dark ribbons of flight.

I shake my head, try to think of another dream, something of comfort, of resolution, to cut off the images that unfold before me, a troubling silent movie. One of the Dissys, from the seventies, swore by iron and copper. A disc of metal to block dreams. The trick never worked for me. Even as I finger the heavy key around my neck, I can feel my Sight uncoiling and writhing in the air around me. And then they come. The wet mud shining underfoot. Trees twisting in the wind, the twig limbs reaching to grab his hand.

"Are you going to choose the final card or should I?" His voice sounds far away.

His hand covers mine and the shock of his touch pulls me from the vision, his dream.

"I know you saw her," he says. "I can see it in your face."

There's no telling what I look like. I want to speak, want to tell him how she hurts and for how long, but the words get stuck in my throat and slide down to the bottom of my belly.

How to tell him that she is lost to him? That the love he seeks is already a dry husk, gone for many seasons.

He must have thought he was reaching back into the past, that she would be as he remembered her, whichever spring it was when their future was green. Who is she? I do not want to know. I just know she does not want him.

\* \* \*

All night, while sleep carries others to dreamland, I work at remembering, rewinding to study others' dreams, to rework the scene. But some signs you do not want to see. I told him a lie because the truth was too expensive. His presence fills the space inside my mind as he sits, arms crossed, legs tucked under him. I breathe through the odor of his sweat and desperation, my back curled, his final card hidden, face down on the table.

When he finally left, I stood on the fire escape, listened to the waves of bachata and kompa music floating up at a sky littered with stars. Night-time. I could still hear the children laugh and leap, shrieking through the darkness below, their shouts mingling with the sharp-edged call of car horns and crows. The ever present crows.

They knew.

The truth I would not admit to myself.

I had told him a sweet lie, a story pieced together of all the women I had ever known. Enough of the truth to make his spirit woman real, enough of a lie to make him release the cards and turn away. A lie stitched together with the threads of past lives, crossed stars, ill-timed fates, the worst kind of luck. Now the crows have come to pick it all apart.

"I'm not going to do it!" I cry. I run out to the terrace, kicking over my poor, struggle herbs. "I don't believe in you."

The black circle slows. The sound comes not from outside, but within my ear. I scream. Regret every foolish word I've uttered. How stupid could I be? The circle of sound reverses itself. The murder of crows dives from the sky, but instead of cutting through the night, they circle inside my head. I back away, knocking over my thyme, and climb back inside. Slam down the window so I cannot hear. They shriek and call, wings clawing at the air. A cloud of them circled overhead, counterclockwise, haranguing me. Their beaks are sharp as needles, sharp enough to pierce the skin.

Bleeding or not, that night I refused to sleep, let alone to dream.

I snatch the cards off the table, hands shaking, I drop one. The Hanged Man, reversed. I stare at the figure entwined in lush green vines, surrounded by blood red flowers and gourd-like fruit, then stuff all the cards into the velvet bag. I double tie it, almost wishing it was a hangman's knot. If only it was that easy. I take the crystals and the bowl of dust and dump them into the trash. A red cloud rises into the air. I am done. D. O. N. E. Done.

I dig in my bra and pull out a couple of the crumpled bills he'd given me and grab my keys. Though I had never been up there before except to get late rent, it was time to see the sock puppets.

I stomp up the rickety stairs so they could hear me coming. The music, propulsive beats that make the whole floor shake, turns down before I even make it to the door.

"What's good?" a sleepy-eyed man asks. He has grown his hair out since last month, and his hair is half-braided. His girl lounges on a couch, frowning in the background. Piles of folded up laundry cover the floor.

"I need to stay awake."

He shakes his head. "Naw, sis, you sure? Look like you need to be sleep."

I hold my money out to him. He won't take it. I dig in my bra and pull out some more. "I don't want to dream."

He turns back to his girl, as if asking permission. She grabs a dress out of the basket and lays it flat across the couch. After she smoothes it out with the palms of her hand, she shrugs. Her purple twists dangle over her shoulders.

"I got you," he says, and disappears into a back room.

* * *

At first there was nothing. I slept the sleep of the ages. So much nothing I could dive into it. Hours and hours of nothingness. I had been resting, better than I had in a good, long while but then, just before dawn, the dreams — if I did not speak them, they would bleed into my waking thoughts.

If I did not speak them, they would tear the veil away from their world into my own, rip and tear at reality, starting with my skin. Soon, nothing gave way to the Sight, the Sight becoming all I could see. The crows came to screech a warning. I had to tell him something. Enough of the truth to keep both him and the spirits away, or I would never have another day or night's peace.

* * *

Real hoodoos, sho'nuff conjurewomen can't be bothered with black cat bones in pockets or meetings at crossroads.

Meetings take place in the mind, in the space where your soul sleeps, where all the signs are newborn, hidden from view. The night after I spent his money, the night after the crows shrieked my name, I hear the house split and crack. I open my eyes and see a zig zag scar across the ceiling above my bed. I watch it grow deeper, longer until I fall asleep. The crack grows while I dream. Then I see him.

"What the hell are you doing here?" I ask.

"What are you doing here?"

We avoid each other's eyes and shift on our sides. He is lying next to me, clutching my pillow as if it's his own. He is dressed in a T-shirt and some tighty-whities. I had pegged him for a boxer man. I'm not looking all that great myself. I am dressed in a jersey tank top that is so tattered, I should have been using it as a dust rag. I clutch myself self-consciously. My best bra is wet, hanging on the shower curtain pole, dripping by the sink. Neither of us admits that we've been keeping our own separate vigils in our sleep. We are so close, almost touching. I assume that this dream is another way for the Dissys to mess with my head, to tease me about latent lust, so I snatch the pillow back from under him.

"Hold up, that's mine," he says when his head bangs against the headboard.

"You're in my dream. My rules."

He looks confused. "Last night, I saw this crack in my wall and I…"

"Put your finger in it and it brought you here. Great. Jacking up my sleep." I snatch the quilt I sleep under year round and cover my boobs like a death shroud. "Go on back where you come from."

"I don't understand…"

He repeats syllables that make no sense to me. All I hear are the sounds of paper peeling back, a window's snap before it cracks, the shift of plaster under layers and layers of paint, the break…

"I'm going back to sleep," he says. "I mean, I'm waking up."

"Boy bye," I say and turn over.

With that he disappears.

\* \* \*

A few nights later we wake to the sound of Mama's house breaking. Before I open my eyes, I know it is him beside me. Of all the people I could dream of waking up to, it's his ass. Not Mama, so I can tell her I'm sorry for not saving her life, for not seeing her dream sooner, not Aunt Dissy or one of the other Dissys, so I can tell them to kiss my ass, not an ex-lover I didn't really want to kick out of the bed, but him. Now I have grown accustomed to his scent. Irish Springs and strong minty toothpaste. He is using mouthwash before he goes to bed. I think I smell the hint of cologne or some kind of dime store aftershave. I am almost flattered that he has started to clean up for me.

He doesn't say anything about my ruined skin. My scars were like tree rings, bloody palm prints, maps of all the horrid dreams I'd ever had. He doesn't stare at them but he doesn't look away either. My scars are my shield. They remind me, even with so much death around, that I still live.

His eyes wonder briefly over the gown I had put on. It is the closest thing to a nightgown I own, and calling it lingerie would be a stretch. I have braided my hair neatly and hid the black satin bonnet I usually sleep with.

We spend the night plastering the cracks, caulking breaks and holes. We think if we make the repairs in our dreams, we will wake to fewer holes in our waking lives. I suspect that neither of us can afford to regularly repair our houses. It sounds like he is almost as broke as I am.

This time the breaking sound is louder. We hope the walls will hold themselves.

I don't know about him, but I definitely cannot afford to move. We clutch our pillows and hold our breath as the sawdust and plaster float down from the ceiling like fairy dust. I'm so tired in this dream, I can barely keep my eyes awake. There is nothing sexy about any of this. My house is dying all around me. It seems like each crack I fill reveals another gaping wound. We are afraid of what the house will do in our sleep, so now we rest in shifts.

When I wake after he's softly snoring, the front wall has moved. The door to my bedroom is gone altogether. Three of the Dissy portraits lay on the floor, facedown, silent as corpses. I panic. I feel trapped. But then I feel cool air tickle my scalp. The ceiling opens up and all the stars look in. I am more surprised at the sight of them than any of the other changes to my room. Suddenly the stars I never see in this city of light and noise and loneliness fill the night sky.

I need a witness. I shake him but he won't wake up. I look for paper and a pen. This is not something I want to write in Aunt Dissy's dream book. This is something I want to keep for myself.

We leave each other notes now. Not love notes . . . just . . . notes.

"The west wall, near the kitchen is going next. I think I heard it rumbling near the bookcase."

"A new set of stairs may appear out of nowhere."

"You overslept! There were more cracks in the hall. I woke to two sets of double doors before I could use the damn bathroom!"

I spend my days at the hardware store. I lug heavy panels, hammers and nails, cans of paint, brushes, and glue. My upstairs tenants don't even bother asking anymore. They know I'm not repairing their shit. They owe me two month's rent and are counting on losing their deposit. And how can I explain? I don't have the heart or the energy to kick them out anyway. I wobble into the brownstone and trip up the stairs, crashing into the walls. Cornrows pokes his head out the door.

"You OK, sis?"

I wave. Now they look at me like *I'm* the fuck up.

I scrape the old paint and smooth out rough edges. I can't remember what my mother's house looked like before, before Aunt Dissy moved in and came to take care of me. The only thing that remains the same are the walls of Dissys. And even they are changing. Their backs are still turned to me, but now I see here and there, a hand on a hip, the jut of a jaw, a bell-shaped hat turned to cover a side-eye in profile. I don't need to see the pictures or their poked out lips to know how much they disapprove.

Our hallways are now labyrinths. I say "our" because he and I now share the same dreaming hell — or purgatory. I can't tell which. We lurch through the house, shoulders stooped, eyes squinted up and frowning.

* * *

After a month of midnight renovations, the full moon returns again. To my surprise, the ravens disappear and the sky is washed clean. I turn away from the mirror and return to my empty bed that is not really empty anymore. I push his pillow over to his side of the bed. By now I know he likes to sleep with his back to the window.

In my dream, I see him as he cannot see himself. The landscapes of his spirit, as level and gentle as an open hand, without one fist for boundary. His goals and joys, memories and defeats are mine now. They lay glittering in small pools of green and brown and gray as he sleeps, continents on a bright unfolding map reaching out, unbroken across the sea.

I see myself, too, reworking a scene that is my own. Not buck naked this time, but wearing the shimmering scraps of clothing like rainbow strips of skin. Instead of running, I'm dancing, and all the breadcrumbs lead back to me.

I think I will tell him someday. On one of these nights when the wind sounds like the rustle of a blackbird's wings, when the stars look sharp enough to slice the black sky into ribbons. I will tell him of Aunt Dissy's book, of all the Dissys who are pretending not to watch us now, and of the woman whose face still holds my unimagined dreams.

\* \* \*

"Aunt Dissy's Policy Dream Book" by Sheree Renée Thomas was originally published in *Apex Magazine*, issue Number 95, and is reprinted with permission. Sheree Renée Thomas is a 2016 Tennessee Arts Fellow and was honored as the 2015 Lucille Geier Lakes Writer-in-Residence at Smith College. Her book, *Shotgun Lullabies: Stories & Poems* (Aqueduct Press, Conversation Pieces Vol. 28) was described by novelist Arthur Flowers as "a wondrous work like Jean Toomer's *Cane*." Her new book, *Sleeping Under the Tree of Life* (Aqueduct Press, Conversation Pieces Vol. 50) received a Starred Review from Publisher's Weekly. A widely published writer and editor, and the first recipient of the 2017 L.A. Banks Award, she is a native of Memphis.

**Joseph B. Atkins / Timothy Ivy Photography**

# THE SINGAPORE HOLY MAN

## BY JOSEPH B. ATKINS

The police in Hong Kong found Michael Bogovin in a brothel in the Wan Chai district, naked and dead under a clean sheet, chest exposed, his head on his pillow as if he were taking a nap, his glass of wine on the bedside table, enough poison still in it to kill anyone tempted to finish it. The police called the poison "Gu", an old Chinese concoction of venom from various snakes and spiders. The whore he'd come to see was missing. She had been with him many times, the madam said. They were lovers. He always insisted on her and on the same room. Was it suicide or murder? No suicide note was found. Where was the woman?

Hong Kong asked Memphis to help. He lived in Memphis part-time, and they found a copy of his round-trip ticket among his clothes. He apparently was important. That is, Mikhail Nechaev, the man who called himself Michael Bogovin.

I pondered all the questions as I watched the sun, a giant, overripe peach, setting across the Mississippi River, soon to slip from view beyond the Arkansas Delta. I watched from my rooftop perch, where I had shared many drinks with Michael Bogovin during his sojourns in what he liked to call "this backwater city of the Old Confederacy." He loved it here, as unlikely as that might seem for someone so worldly and sophisticated. Apparently Memphis was the perfect hiding place for Michael Bogovin.

The last drink I had with him was just last month, the night before he left. I drank bourbon. He drank vodka. His mind was already far away. One could hear the rumble of the trolleys from the street below. After a long silence, he pulled something from inside his jacket. A small book, red cloth with gold binding. It was locked, and he gave me the key.

"I want to leave this with you," he said. "Not to read — that is, unless I fail to return — but to keep. I don't want it to be lost. Hong Kong is a city where you can lose anything, including your life. Tell no one you have it."

He laughed. He was a tall, lean man with a base-baritone laugh that I didn't hear often. "I've become superstitious, like an old Russian who believes in signs and Tarot cards, gypsy prophecies." I never knew this, and my surprise showed. "Yes, Joseph, that's me. Afraid of what might be rather than what is."

Then he told me something I'd been told before. "I'll be bringing you back a story, by the way. The story of a lifetime."

The police don't know about the diary. I told them what he said about Hong Kong.

That last evening with him reminded me of how little I knew about my rooftop companion. He was a businessman who traveled, a Russian who had been in this country many years, a frustrated writer who was much better at business, secretive but affable, given to occasional tales of distant lands but rarely including himself in those tales.

He knew much more about me, or thought he did. I was the writer he never became, or so he said. This flattered and amused me, but he was wrong, and I tried to tell him. I was an old, disgraced hack who had spent much of his life shoving out reams of copy against deadline, a hack who finally decided he'd had enough and did what reporters like to claim but rarely do: tell the truth. No sooner did I begin busting the business suits behind the crooked pols than I crashed faster than Icarus.

I took another sip of my bourbon and picked up the diary. It was time to read it. He had only made a few entries, all in English. No dates. Each entry on a separate page.

\* \* \*

*"You are a good man who does bad things"*

*Those were the words I heard soon after crossing the Bras Basah Road on my way back to my hotel. I've heard them a thousand times since in my thoughts and in my dreams.*

*I had just spent a couple hours at the museum, an exhibition of realism in modern Asian art. The sun outside was blinding. The young man who was to say those words stood on the other side of the road. He seemed an apparition – thin, dark-skinned, his clothes mere rags, a beggar.*

*"Pardon me, sir," he cried out to me as I walked past him and the Cathedral of the Good Shepherd. "I must speak with you."*

*He was persistent and followed me. I stopped. I don't know why. It was my last day in Singapore. I had dark feelings about leaving. He caught up with me and smiled. "Thank you, sir. I saw your face, and I had to speak with you."*

*He fished a scrap of paper and worn pencil out of a pocket and scribbled something on it. Then he carefully folded it several times into a neat square and placed it in my hand. "You may think me silly, sir, but please tell me your favorite color?"*

*I shook my head. I had far too much time on my hands. I wasn't even sure of the answer. A Russian might say red. An American green. I said blue.*

*"Please look at the piece of paper."*

*On the paper was written the word "blue". I was mildly impressed until I decided blue is probably what most people would say. Still, his trick deserved a reward. I found a couple Singapore dollars to give him, but he held up his hand and waved them away. "No, no, no, sir. I only did this to prove to you I see into the mind. And, sir, I see into the soul as well. I am a holy man, a man who seeks peace, and I see in you a great unrest."*

*He was right, of course, again, but isn't there "a great unrest" in everyone? What was it Philo said? "Be kind, for everyone is fighting a great battle." I turned to leave. He stopped me. "Your eyes tell me, sir, that you have trouble sleeping, that things buried inside you come out at night, many demons. They make you lie awake for hours. If I am wrong, you may walk away, sir."*

*I didn't, and he smiled again under intense brown eyes. "You are a good man, sir, but a good man who does bad things." He reached into another pocket, pulled out a small medallion, and mouthed some words over it. It was blue with an arcane design on it. He pressed it into the same hand where he had placed the paper. "Take this, a blessing. Keep it close to you. It has power over evil. It will keep you from the bad things." I stepped back, and he touched my sleeve. "I only want peace for you, sir. This is my mission."*

*I looked down at the medallion. It had passed through many hands. A strange artifact for me to remember this last visit to Singapore. I pushed it back into his pocket. "Keep your lucky charm, holy man. Shalom."*

*As I walked away, I felt his eyes bearing down on me. Indeed, at the corner where Bras Basah meets Victoria, I looked back, and he hadn't moved. His arms hung to his side like the most pathetic of beggars, and he was mouthing silent words again.*

\* \* \*

The Memphis police let me see his apartment. I had never been inside it before. It was filled with a curious mix of second-hand furniture, likely purchased from those antique-and-junk stores along Summer Avenue, and brand new dining room and bedroom sets. Books lined the shelves in his office, many old and yellowed, books about Asia, Hinduism, Buddhism, the Russian monk St. Seraphim of Sarov. A well-thumbed Russian Bible was on his nightstand. His refrigerator was nearly empty, but in the cupboard next to it were tins of caviar and a basket of chocolate bars. On the counter was an unopened bottle of a rare Georgian wine impossible to purchase in Memphis or any place beyond Russia and the Black Sea.

They showed me the trunk they found next to a stack of newspapers in one of the closets. Inside were piles of Rolex watches, iPhones, MP3 players, expensive perfumes, jewelry, and stacks of cash in multiple currencies.

* * *

*I never gave another thought to the holy man from Singapore, even in my hotel room as I tore at my sheet with the usual nightmares, even on the flight the next morning to Beijing as a storm over the South China Sea rocked us violently from side to side, spilling our champagne and caviar across the floor, forcing the woman in the seat next to me to take out her rosary and pray not to die.*

*When we finally arrived, I quickly got to my little courtyard in the Hutong, went to my bedroom, emptied my pockets, unpacked a few things, and began making calls. A meeting was scheduled for early the next morning. I needed sleep but I had no time to waste. I was so busy I almost missed the blue medallion that was lying with my change next to the Dorje Drolo on my table.*

*I picked it up. It was the holy man's medallion. How could it be? I had clearly shoved the thing back in the man's pocket. Had he somehow slipped it back into mine? That had to be what happened. The Singapore holy man was a persistent beggar indeed, yet a strange beggar who gives rather than receives?*

*I studied it, noticing for the first time tiny calligraphy under the design, then I tossed it in a drawer with my Singapore change. I would take it out again many times.*

\* \* \*

"Watcha readin'?"

I closed the book and turned to see Memphis police detective Sam Belk staring down at me, smiling under his walrus mustache. We'd spoken several times over the past week. He'd okayed me seeing Michael's apartment. He looked like a lot of Southern cops I had known during my years as a reporter--overweight, slumping shoulders, careworn face, big feet. A certain flair was in the mustache and twinkling, intelligent eyes, however. It told of a man who had learned not to take the world too seriously.

"A journal. Every writer has one. You can get great stories from an old journal."

He pulled out a chair and sat heavily. A lit filtered Marlboro followed. "Thought you didn't chase stories any more."

"Old reporters are always chasing stories, most of them in their dreams."

Belk took a long drag and watched a barge make its way downriver. "Old cops are the same. Chasin' bad guys in their dreams. I gotta call from Hong Kong today. Looks like they've lost interest in your Russian friend, told me to drop the matter, that it's been ruled a suicide, and, well, that's that, all she wrote."

He offered me a cigarette, and I took it. We both watched the barge pass under the Old Bridge in the dimming light. "Funny thing. They were all excited a week ago. This Bogo-vine-Netch-ov was a well-connected man, they said, a man with influential friends, and they suspected foul play. Now all of a sudden, it's no big deal."

"Did the woman show up? The prostitute?"

"Nope. I asked. Not important, they said. Just another Hong Kong whore."

"Hmmmm ... ."

"My sentiments exactly."

I shook the ice cubes left from my last drink. "That time again. Can I get you one?"

He checked his watch. It was pushing eight. "You know, it has been a long day. A long week."

A question came to mind as I stood up. "By the way, who let you in this building? You got a key or something?"

A smile stretched across his broad face. "I know your guy in the lobby. Used to be on the force."

I left Michael's journal in my apartment before returning with bourbons for both of us. I had known Belk as a cop in uniform many years before. I met him while working on a story retracing Abe Fortas' ties to Boss Crump and the Hoodoo Cartel, and he led me to some decades-old files the chief had under lock and key. Belk was a different breed even then, a cop willing to bend the rules for something other than himself.

"Did I ever tell you you look like Nietzsche with that mustache?"

He downed the bourbon and eyed his empty glass thoughtfully. "What doesn't kill you makes you stronger."

"A catchy phrase. I'll remember that."

A cop who knows Nietzsche. A different breed all right. "I gotta another question about this case. Why does a man buy a round-trip ticket if he's planning to commit suicide?"

"Surprised that wasn't your first question. You must be slipping. Not the young newshound I helped taint the memory of a former Supreme Court justice, who wasn't that bad a fellow, by the way. Michael Bo-go-vine was a strange one, a man of many names. They're not even sure Netch-ov is the one he was born with."

"Why buy new furniture for your apartment if you're planning to end it all?"

"That's another worthy question."

Michael intended to return, meant to collect his diary, knew he might not live to do it.

Belk stretched his legs and rested his hands on his belly. "The department is tickled to drop this thing. Got zero interest and plenty else to do. This is a guy who was passing through, not a local. Me, I'm curious. Who was this fellow? Why go to Hong Kong to cash in? Hell, why not here with all the rest of the insulted and injured at the bottom of Big Muddy? Memphis has plenty of prostitutes, too, who'd be more than happy to spend your last night with you."

The insulted and injured. Does the cop know Dostoevsky, too? "Maybe he decided to do it after he got to Hong Kong."

"And went to the corner pharmacy and bought some Gu, right?"

Belk stood up and assessed the rooftop view of Main Street, the Friday night crowds below, the neon at the Peabody and Orpheum, the trolley lights, horse-drawn carriages lit up like Chinese New Year dragons. "Nice," he said and turned to go. "Thanks for the drink. Let's talk again."

"Sure, anytime," I said and tipped my glass in his direction.

Suicides don't buy round-trip tickets. I finished my drink. I had some more reading to do.

\* \* \*

*I read a story once by the writer Maugham. It was about an Irishman named Gallagher who died at sea of hiccups, a curse given him by his abandoned Malaysian mistress. Perhaps my blue medallion was a curse, not a good luck charm. I laughed, the good man who does bad things.*

*A good man indeed. Like Saul of Tarsus, hunting down the Christians, beating them, spitting on them, selling them into slavery. The zealot who watched the Jews stone Stephen and approved. Gave them the stones, held their cloaks.*

*Saul in a business suit in a boardroom with Herod and Caiphas, both in business suits, too, marking their deals with toasts of Maotai, over drawings of factories where the slaves are grateful for a bowl of watery rice, an occasional stuffed bun, and only know they're slaves after it's too late. Saul serving Pontius Pilate, with his immaculate hands and incessant demands for more silver.*

*However, this Saul, too, was struck down on his road to Damascus, made to see his blindness. This was not long after Singapore. God used a woman named Wyen to open this Saul's eyes, a slave herself, sold to a Babel Saul had once toasted, a fugitive captured and sold again until she found her last refuge, a whorehouse in a strange city where no one spoke her language or cared about her past. That is, until she lay with Saul himself and removed the scales from his eyes.*

\* \* \*

I stopped to fix another drink. A double shot straight on ice. I'd regret it in the morning, but maybe not so much. No more wife there to nag me. No more editor there to curse me. Just me, thanks to a long-legged blonde in the front office who meant nothing to me, and to a source who promised a document, turned chicken, and I went with the story anyway. Big mistake.

Only one more entry in the diary, and I decided to savor what I had read before finishing. Michael should have given himself more credit. He had the Russian genius for telling a story, but what did it mean? I never knew he was religious. The Bible by his bed had been a surprise, like all this talk about Saul. I guessed he would be Paul in the final entry, preaching to the gentiles, running for his life from his old bosses. The bourbon opened a synapse, and I began to re-appreciate Michael's tale. The Jews killed Paul, right? I must have skipped Father Nathaniel's lesson that day down in Greenwood. I looked around my apartment. Not a Bible in sight.

* * *

*I walked away from that whorehouse thinking of what Paul once said. "I am carnal, sold into slavery to sin. What I do, I do not understand. For I do not what I want, but I do what I hate." I was determined to free myself, the woman who had made me see, and all the other slaves I had sent into charnel houses. This was when I remembered the holy man from Singapore and his blue medallion. "It will keep you from the bad things," he told me. So it was not a curse after all! It was what the holy man had said it was. A blessing! I was drunk with my newfound freedom, and I vowed to make preparations for a new life for me and Wyen.*

*Still, this was a blessing that brought with it great danger. No master willingly releases his slave, and he will not tolerate those who threaten what is his.*

* * *

This was all he wrote. It wasn't much of a diary. More a confession than a diary. Enough, however. He had told what he could of his story. His writer friend would have to tell the rest of it. I looked at the clock. It was midnight. Belk would be awake. He was like me, divorced, alone, probably with a drink in his hand. I rang his number.

"We need to talk."

* * *

I met Belk at the front door of my apartment building at nine the next morning. He suggested breakfast at Bon-Ton, his dime. It was just around the corner on Monroe. I hadn't been there since it came under new ownership.

"I used to come here when I was a beat cop, drink coffee with Papa from the Old Country," he said as the waiter filled our cups. "He knew everybody in the neighborhood, high and low. I owe that Greek my career. Never gave me a bad tip. Long time ago."

Belk was pokerfaced as I told him about the diary, what was in it, and my latest theory, finalized while shaving that morning. "He wrote it in English, not Russian. He wanted someone — me — to be able to read it. None of it's dated. I think he wrote it after the fact, to get it down on paper, and he knew it might be a last testament."

The coffee was strong. Papa would be proud.

"Michael never talked much about himself. Of course, an old reporter asks a lot of questions. He wouldn't answer most of them, but I picked up a few things. He grew up in Brezhnev's Russia, hated those hammer and sickle days, blamed them for the loss of his family."

"When did he get religion?"

"Not sure he did, not before that trip to Singapore. I didn't know that side of Michael Bogovin. He liked to ask me about it, me who's been in mortal sin most of his life. He loved hearing about Father Nathaniel in Greenwood, though."

"I remember Father Nathaniel. I got folks down there."

"I remember us discussing that long time ago. If Michael got religion, maybe it was a kind of rebellion against the crap they preached in the Young Pioneers."

Belk nodded. "That makes sense." I looked at him with admiration. He knew who the hell the Young Pioneers were. I remembered similar admiration back when I was looking into Abe Fortas' career. Belk knew enough history to want to help me.

He thanked me for telling him about the diary. "I have to admit I've been holding back a bit myself, so let me tell you a few things. A couple friends of mine in Washington helped me find out about this Bogo-vine-Netch-ov. He was a pretty fascinating fellow. Seems his real name was Nekrasov. Spoke Cantonese and Mandarin as well as Russian and English. French, too. Smart. He came to the States as a young man during the chaos of the Yeltsin years. His parents had been what my friends call `party apparat-check' but got caught up in Kremlin politics and disappeared. Probably sent to Siberia and died there."

"That's apparatchik. Chick, like little chicken, like cute girl."

"If you say so. Young Michael stayed behind, got himself a good education, and left the new free Russia at the first opportunity. He came to the States — Brighton Beach, to be exact--where he learned to be as good a capitalist as his parents were communists. My friends aren't sure who greased the skids, but he got some help somewhere and moved up the ranks quickly as a kind of free-wheeling business agent."

"All those trips to Asia … ."

"That's right. No clue where he learned Chinese, but they say it gets easier the more languages you know. He wasn't just well-connected in Hong Kong. Brighton Beach ain't that far from Wall Street, and he was about as slick as that fellow Michael Douglas played in the movie. He made good money being Bogo-vine here, Netch-ov in Hong Kong and New York, and Nekrasov back in Moscow. My friends are still checking the details of how he made money, and maybe where that money is. Our government has a file on him, of course. They knew who he was."

"And didn't care, it seems."

"Naw, he was doing god's work, and you know who god is on Wall Street. Capitol Hill for that matter"

"Then came Singapore …."

"And his lady friend in Hong Kong. Don't figure things started there, though. Troubles like that brew a long time. A man will keep doing things contrary to his nature for years before he decides enough's enough."

Belk gave me a world-weary look over that drooping Nietzsche mustache. I raised my cup and tipped his.

"The question is: What was he doing?"

\* \* \*

Belk wouldn't tell me who his friends in Washington were. He only promised to keep me posted. He knew he had whetted my appetite, though. And he knew I knew he knew. I wanted to see Michael's apartment again, check out those newspapers, that treasure trove in the trunk. He told me to come down to the station.

The station was a short walk, and I found Belk outside the building entrance with other smokers enjoying a nicotine break. He led me inside to his office, which was about the size of a walk-in closet. In the corner were the trunk and a wooden crate holding the Russian Bible, the Georgian wine, several books, and the newspapers. I looked around. On the desk in his cluttered office was a framed picture of a middle-aged woman and two teenaged boys. I picked it up. The older boy looked like Belk.

"She remarried and moved to Atlanta. The boys call her husband `Dad'. They hardly know me. I was never around."

I nodded. "I lost mine before we could produce progeny. In fact, that was one of the problems."

He shrugged and pointed to the stack of papers. "Use my chair and look all you want. I asked to keep this stuff for a while. Nobody here cares. We got his furniture in storage till we figure out what to do with it. I think your landlord already has a new renter lined up for his apartment. I got other business to tend. Take your time."

What I found was a mix of Asian and Western newspapers, in English and some in Chinese — the *South China Morning Post, Beijing Times, International Herald Tribune,* the *Wall Street Journal's* Asian edition. A curious chronology of death existed among them. Most headlined stories going back years on factories fires, ammonia leaks, collapsed multi-level buildings, slaughterhouses with hundreds dead or injured, incinerated in human infernos, buried under tons of low-grade cement and iron rods, trapped behind doors bolted to keep them from taking unauthorized breaks. Along with the stories were photographs of dead, weeping or angry Chinese, many in the pink overalls and blue aprons workers wear. One long tale of woe and malfeasance.

"`Let me out! Let me out! For God's sake, let me out!'" poultry worker Yao Zong heard a trapped fellow worker scream at a poultry plant fire in Jilin province. Yao said he could do nothing but watch helplessly. "The fire was so strong I couldn't get to him." Yao was in an adjoining warehouse when the explosion took place. The plant doors were bolted. They were always bolted before and after the lunch break.

I looked up from the newspaper. The Chinese cry to God, too? I didn't know that. Like most everybody else, they die waiting for an answer.

Over the next two hours I traveled via the newspapers an industrial corridor that stretches from Jilin province in northern China to Dongguan in southeast China's Guangdong province, from Phnom Penh, Cambodia, to as far away as Dhaka, Bangladesh. Whether the factories processed chicken or made clothes, toys or computer parts, they served their masters from Hong Kong, Singapore, Taipei, New York, Silicon Valley, and backwoods Arkansas. I was exhausted at the end, as if I had actually been to those factories.

I didn't have Michael's diary with me, but I remembered what was in it. *Saul in a business suit in a boardroom with Herod and Caiphas, both in business suits, too, marking their deals with toasts of Maotai, over drawings of factories where the slaves are grateful for a bowl of watery rice, an occasional stuffed bun, and only know they're slaves after it's too late.*

I spent another half-hour going through the trunk and all its goodies — the Rolex watches, jewelry, MP3 players, tools of the trade, the kinds of baubles that open doors, put people in a friendly mood.

Michael, the good man who did bad things, was the agent who put Herod and Pontius Pilate, or their representatives, in the same room, raised his glass to toast their deals, and got rich off his commissions. He was Saul all right. Then a Singapore holy man and a Hong Kong whore made the blind see.

Just as I stood up to stretch, Belk returned. An unlit Marlboro dangled between his lips. "Damned shame you can't smoke in an office you worked thirty years to occupy. Pleasant reading?"

"Have you read 'em?"

"Of course. They give you any ideas what he was doing?"

"Come up to the rooftop this evening. Let's talk about it. Drinks are free."

\* \* \*

The sky had turned black by the time Belk showed up. Not a moon nor a star, just a gathering of big, heavy clouds. I was on my third drink and had one ready for him although the ice had melted. He didn't care.

"I've got some ideas about what happened to Michael, but I'd like to hear your impressions of that collection in your office first."

"Same as yours, I'm sure, but I've been talking to my friends again. Seems Netch-ov was a middle man helping U.S. firms in Asia, finding suppliers who could make their products on the cheap, a dealmaker who spoke the language of the natives, a tough guy Russian who drove the kind of hard bargain the boys in the boardrooms love and the local yokels hate, a high-paid free-lancer who got the job done and to hell with all the rest."

The first sprinkle of rain began to fall. More was coming. "Let's shift down to my apartment. Wanna share with you my thoughts."

* * *

Belk assessed my place with no comment. He did ask for ice and a refresher, however. I continued.

"Hong Kong says Michael was well-connected, important. I believe it. A guy in his business has to know a lot of people, and, like you said, accumulates a few enemies along the way. He's not only dealing with business types, he's dealing with government officials, too, people who are either in on the deal or looking the other way."

"Sounds like Memphis."

"Neither one of us are ever going to figure out what happened to Michael Bogovin sitting here in Memphis, Tennessee. That's why I'm going to Hong Kong."

His eyes twinkled as he settled in his chair to enjoy what was coming next.

"What the hell do you know about Hong Kong?"

"Been there. I was in Vietnam, took R&R in Hong Kong. Picked up the clap there but otherwise enjoyed it immensely."

"Maybe your whore was his whore's mama," he said, and we both had a chuckle. "Look, I know you were a hotshot reporter back in the day. Otherwise I'd have never risked my career slipping you information like I did. But, my friend, you ain't been in Hong Kong in forty years. What you figure? You just going to land, find that house of joy where you got the clap and start from there?"

He knew better. He was riding me. Belk was tickled I was going to Hong Kong. Maybe he even expected it. I had the kind of savings account a man with no obligations can build, finally had a reason to dip into it.

"You know, you're still a hotshot even if that bad egg messed you up."

My downfall was no secret to Belk. He'd even worked with me on the story. "Messed me up all right. If he'd produced that letter he promised, Memphis' Businessman of the Year would be in jail, and a couple of his politician friends, too."

"And you'd have a job."

"Even hotshots learn their lesson."

"Who was he, by the way?"

"You know better than that."

"I'd of been disappointed had you told me. I'll give you a name, though. Timothy Cheung, the officer we talked to in Hong Kong. I looked it up before I came over here. Figured you might need to know."

\* \* \*

The twenty-one-hour flight from Memphis to Hong Kong, with layovers in Chicago and Tokyo, offered plenty of time to think. The newspapers Michael had collected reminded me of a poultry plant fire I had covered in North Carolina in the early 1990s. Twenty-five dead behind locked doors. Those stories were always the same. Lots of excuses, denials, and funerals. Michael's confession was a first.

I wondered why I was on that plane. For Michael? For the story he promised? To redeem myself? Maybe it was all of those things.

Even though I was sandwiched between a fussy, demanding scion of China's one-child policy and an overweight American with sleep apnea, the long flight also gave me time to read the book Michael owned about St. Seraphim of Sarov, a 19th century Russian monk who fed wild bears and prayed on a rock for a thousand days and nights. The saint preached "peace of soul," and he could see into souls and determine whether there was peace or unrest there. Had the Singapore holy man been some sort of reincarnation?

Michael and I had hit it off first time we met. Each of us saw something in the other missing in ourselves. I envied his freedom. No bosses yanking his chain. Off to some exotic port on a moment's notice. Memphis was his escape. For me, Memphis was the end of the road, I once told him. No better place for a writer, he said.

As dog tired as I was when we landed at the Hong Kong airport on Lantau Island, the cab ride to the Hotel Far East at the southern tip of Nathan Road in Kowloon was a revelation. The colonial-era buildings in the Central District had disappeared behind a wall of skyscrapers. Spotting a Chinese junk in Victoria Harbor was about as likely as finding my old girlfriend at the Suzie Wong Bar in Wan Chai.

I had a simple plan and seven days to execute it. A lot of questions needed answering besides the obvious one. Was there an autopsy? Where was Michael buried? What about his place in Beijing, his other belongings? A week-long effort before departure trying to set up interviews had produced no response from the Hong Kong police or Timothy Cheung. The only confirmation came from the China Labour Monitor on Ta Kok Tsui Road near my hotel. The NGO was cited in several of the articles. Its job was to serve the people described in those newspaper stories in Belk's office. It kept a sharp eye on Pontius Pilate and Herod in this part of the world and just might know a few things about Saul of Tarsus, too.

The bed in my room was as hard as a coroner's slab, but three Bombays at the lobby bar helped ease me into a troubled sleep filled with dreams from Vietnam and 1972 Hong Kong, where my buddy Bobby Vann predicted on the last day we were there, "We'll never see this place again." I dreamed of Michael Bogovin, too, the Gu sliding through his veins, telling him just before it shut down his heart that this is what his conversion got him. That is, unless somebody did something about it.

James Crowther, the communications specialist with the China Labour Monitor, was an Englishman, fortyish, thin, dark shirt, off-white slacks. We were in what looked like their bull session room. A large blackboard stretched across the wall behind him, and it was filled with handwritten Chinese calligraphy and English acronyms, all connected into some sort of chart, some of it circled in red. Boxes lined the wall beneath the blackboard. I explained I was a journalist researching plant accidents in China and elsewhere in Asia. Then I brought up Michael, said he was a connecting factor.

"He helped corporations in the West find the bottom-feeders, the suppliers that deliver and don't get choked up on scruples. I want to know more about him."

Crowther's friendly demeanor went cold. "What makes you think I would know Mikhail Nechaev?" He fidgeted. "I wish I could help but I don't think I can."

He was hiding something. He filled the next fifteen minutes with questions to me. He wanted to be certain I was who I said I was, asked to see my press ID. I no longer had any. I didn't even have a business card. He studied my passport like he was a customs officer and signaled the interview was at an end.

I finally confessed I was Michael's friend and I wanted to find out who murdered him. He only stared at me. As he led me to the door, I gave him the name of my hotel.

My other interviews didn't fare much better. The woman at the Mission for Migrant Workers at St. John's Cathedral in the Central District even asked the name of the corporation that had hired me. "I'm a free-lance journalist. I don't work for a corporation," I told her. As with Crowther, I finally told her my real purpose. In Hong Kong were many women named Wyen, she said.

These were the good guys. I worried what the rest of the

week had in store.

The next day was no better. The police continued to stall me, as did the U.S.-Hong Kong Business Chamber. Calls to the city's leading police watchdog outfit were unreturned. The archives at the *South China Morning Post* had not one word about Michael. The editor I talked with smiled, offered me coffee, even called one of his police reporters to ask him about Michael. No luck. "Hong Kong is a big city, Mr. Wolfe," the editor said, a hint of condescension in his impeccable English. "People die every day. They die of poison, gunshot wounds, heart attacks, old age, breathing Hong Kong air. So many die with us paying no attention to them. It is very sad."

I returned to the hotel that night a failure. Maybe I was totally out of my league. I had been a reporter for nearly forty years, six of them in Washington, most of them in the South, occasionally an assignment in Mexico or Europe. Still, international intrigue was not my beat. "What the hell was I thinking?" I asked the waitress at the hotel bar when she brought me my fourth Bombay-and-tonic. She smiled.

Everybody smiles in this damned place, I groused to myself, but nobody tells you a thing.

The phone in my room started ringing just as I struggled to get the card in its slot so I could unlock the door.

"There's a tea shop on the first floor of the Mariners' Club around the corner from your hotel," Crowther said from the other end of the line. "Meet me there at ten in the morning."

I punched the mattress a half-dozen times to create some give, but it was stubborn. No matter. I slept like a baby.

\* \* \*

Crowther was waiting when I arrived. The tearoom was dark, intimate, a place where the waiter brought your tea and disappeared behind a bamboo curtain. In the quiet you could hear singing upstairs. Ten o'clock mass at St. Peter's.

"If Mikhail weren't dead, I wouldn't be talking to you," Crowther said, speaking just above a whisper even though no one was in earshot. "His relationship to us and to others like us is what got him in trouble. He was incredible. He had records of all their secret deals, and when he began feeding us information, we were aware of the danger. Someone tried to kill him earlier this year. He was crossing Chatham Road, near the museum, and a car sped out of nowhere and tried to run over him. He was being followed. He once told me he had a journalist friend in the States he was going to tell everything. When you contacted me, I wondered if you were he, but I couldn't be sure. Their spies are everywhere."

"I was beginning to think I made this trip for nothing."

"I don't know if they're aware of you or not, but they will be if you keep asking questions."

"Who are `they'?"

"The ones who poisoned Mikhail. My list of suspects is long."

"The Chinese?

"He was a man on a mission, and his killers found out about it."

"Where is the woman, the prostitute?"

"Where they can't find her, let us hope. They would love to know."

"I have to find out. Maybe she worked for them."

I asked for the location of the brothel and the name of its madam. He advised against going there. I insisted. He told how Michael had documents exposing a secret network of businessmen, government officials, cops, friendly journalists, and labor leaders who played both sides of the fence. Still, Michael never revealed who his actual clients were, which deals he himself had helped seal, nothing about his own sources.

"He was a goldmine of information that we'll be using for years. We had to respect his rules, however. He was risking his life. You're a journalist. You know how this works. This is why this conversation never happened."

I nodded. I had a lifetime of training in conversations that never happened.

\* \* \*

Wan Chai is a long, gaudy stretch of strip clubs, American bars, whorehouses and massage parlors. Even midday, women in tight, sleeveless black dresses with hemlines just below the buttocks were at nearly every corner or on the arm of sixty-year-old Americans or Englishmen. Music boomed from inside the bars, competing with the honking and chatter in the street. The brothel where Michael died was in an alley and up a green staircase with advertisements in both Chinese and English on every step.

Crowther said ask for Vicky. She was the madam.

A young woman with thick eyelashes and a blond wig led me inside to a waiting room bathed in the same soft, red light you see in movies about places like this. On the wall was a Renoir nude enjoying her bath. Vicky didn't keep me waiting long. She was tall for a Chinese, the presence of a woman in charge, stylish black qipao, red hair like Renoir's bather. I gave it to her straight. I was Mikhail Nechaev's friend. I wanted to know what happened. I wanted to talk to Wyen.

"Wyen no longer here." Her eyes searched my face. "Gone. Never come back maybe."

It was the answer I expected. "I'm not here to get her in trouble. I've come a long way. My friend deserved better."

I produced a roll of bills. She took it.

"Mikhail my friend too. What happened bad. For me, for everyone. I help you find Wyen."

I left wondering whether this had been another dead end.

\* \* \*

Hong Kong police inspector Timothy Cheung listened patiently as I explained my relationship to Mikhail Nechaev-Michael Bogovin and my desire to know the details of what happened to my friend, where he is buried, the autopsy report.

Mildly impressed that I had traveled all the way from the U.S. to inquire about a routine suicide, Cheung said Nechaev had been cremated, his ashes stored in one of the columbaria at Hong Kong Cemetery. "Happy Valley, near racetrack." He assured me he would forward my request for a copy of the autopsy report to the coroner's office.

I left police headquarters and went straight to the sprawling hilltop cemetery. Michael's ashes hadn't arrived. The coroner still had them.

Unscheduled stops at two more NGOs, a trade group, and even a Russian Orthodox church produced only a couple promises to get back to me. To be such a well-connected man, Mikhail Nechaev certainly kept his name and his connections out of the limelight.

* * *

It was my last day, and I had little to show for my week in the city. When I returned to the hotel, however, the concierge told me a woman had left a note in a red envelope. "Meet 7 tonite. Graham street Soho. Turkish bar."

I called a cab and told the driver to step on it. We had less than twenty minutes to get to the other side of Hong Kong.

A sudden downpour blurred the view from the backseat of the cab as it climbed the steep hills of Soho, past crowds racing for shelter among the sea of bars and restaurants. The cab stopped in front of a place called Old Istanbul. It was at an intersection and nearly hidden behind an outside stairwell that connected Graham with streets above and below. The stairwell was thick with people escaping the rain.

Inside Old Istanbul a young woman wearing a waist-length dark jacket and blue jeans waited alone at the end of the bar. I sat down next to her. She was hardly more than a silhouette in the shadows. The only light came from a small lamp with a red shade. Her hair was cut short, like a boy's.

I gave her the note. "My name is Wolfe, Joe Wolfe. Is this yours?"

"Identification, please." She looked at my passport and glanced toward the door. "Mike talk about you. He trust you."

I pulled out the diary. She held it to the lamp and read a few pages. She handed it back to me and wiped her eyes.

"I gave him this. A present. He died because of what I give you." At her feet between the stool and the bar was a satchel.

Her face came into the light. No wonder Michael fell in love with her. She was beautiful. She told how Michael was going to take her to America, bring down the people who had sold her into slavery, devote his life to working against the evil he had once served. The evil included Madam Vicky, who had brought them the wine that poisoned him. Wyen was supposed to drink it, too, but Michael stopped her. He knew after only a couple swallows.

"How did you know to contact me?"

She reached for the handbag. "You leave. Take this. Go back to America."

I smelled jasmine as I leaned over and kissed her on the cheek. "Let me help you, Wyen. Your life is in danger."

"I have friends who protect me."

I insisted on calling her a cab.

As soon as we stepped out the door of Old Istanbul, a shot rang out from somewhere in the night and just missed her. We ran in the opposite direction, taking a side street that plunged downward into a maze of yellow and green signs and red construction barriers.

Another shot whizzed past us, and we ducked through

the door of a church. Hundreds of young women, Filipinas, were crowded together to hear mass. More were entering from the main door to our right, and they packed the tiny space in front of a dark-skinned priest in green and white vestments.

"He had been a sinner like us all, Jews and gentiles," the priest told his congregation, "and he preached redemption. He died at the hands of Nero, the gentile emperor, legend has it. Yet Paul spoke truth, not only for his times but ours as well."

A disturbance was taking place at the main entrance, people shouting, pushing up against one another, and I saw two men in dark suits shoving their way inside. I grabbed Wyen and we made our way back to the door we entered. The alley was empty, and we ran toward the construction barriers below. A third shot roared, however, and Wyen fell onto the asphalt with a sharp cry. I reached down to grab her. The bullet had nicked her shoulder just below her neck. Blood quickly pooled, but the wound was superficial.

She got up to a crouch and pulled me down a stairway and into the blackness of another alley. We soon heard the men rush past us.

"You must go!" she said. "No worry. They never find me. Take what I give you. You will know what to do."

I resisted. "They found you tonight."

"They find you," she said. "Then me."

"Come."

I grabbed her and the bag, and we ran down the alley toward the street lights at the end. She loosened her hand at one point, and when I turned she was gone. I called out to her, but there was no answer.

\* \* \*

Everything began to come together at 35,000 feet somewhere between Hong Kong and Chicago. I poured through the documents at my window seat. Among them was a statement from a Memphis bank account Michael had created in my name. It had a six-figure balance. The other documents — copies of bills of sale, contracts, signed letters, tax statements--told a modern-day story of greed and corruption as old as the Bible. Saul-turned-Paul had gotten the goods on the dealmakers and slave-makers. As I read, I thought of the priest in the church where Wyen and I hid. Nero killed Paul. The Romans, not the Jews. The same was true for Michael. I was sure of it, and I would tell the world.

I had my story. This was not one story. This was a thousand stories. My source delivered his documents this time. Michael had even gotten me a safe deposit box at the Memphis bank. More documents were in it, I was certain.

I would return to Hong Kong. Michael knew I would, and he made it possible. I would see Wyen again. It wasn't hard to figure out who told her about me.

I closed the satchel that held the documents and reached in my coat pocket for the key. I never returned to the hotel so I was wearing the same clothes I had worn running through Soho's streets. The key was there, and something else, too. I held it up to the window and studied it, the arcane design, the tiny calligraphy under the design. She must have slipped it in my pocket.

"That some sort of rare coin," my neighbor in the aisle seat asked.

I shook my head. "A gift from a holy man in Singapore. It keeps you from doing bad things."

The man chuckled. "I could use one of those."

* * *

"The Singapore Holy Man" by Joseph B. Atkins is published for the first time in *Mojo Rising* with permission of the author. Atkins is a veteran writer and professor of journalism at the University of Mississippi. His novel *Casey's Last Chance* (Sartoris Literary Group, 2015) was praised by Edgar Award winning novelist Megan Abbott as "pitch-perfect vintage noir." A North Carolina native and former congressional correspondent, Atkins is also author of *Covering for the Bosses: Labor and the Southern Press* (University Press of Mississippi) and editor of two published collections of essays. His short stories have appeared in *Alfred Hitchcock Mystery Magazine* and *Hardboiled.*

# *In Memoriam*

We end this book with a story by the late Larry Brown, a former Marine, lumberjack, hay hauler, and house painter who was working as a firefighter in Oxford, Mississippi, when he began writing his amazing short stories. After his first collection was published, *Facing the Music* (Algonquin Books, 1988), he continued to write stories, novels, and works of nonfiction until his death at fifty-three in 2004. His novel *Big Bad Love* was made into a film starring Debra Winger, and his novel *Joe* was made into a film starring Nicholas Cage. The story that follows comes from his 2000 novel *Fay*. In his all-too-short life, Brown embodied the continuing literary richness of the Mojo Triangle.

**Larry Brown / Photo courtesy Algonquin Books**

# GIRL ON THE ROAD

## BY LARRY BROWN

In pockets of their own shade the trees stood clumped along the pasture fence and a hot wind stirred the grass at her feet. The concrete was throwing the heat of the sun back into her face after only two hours. She could hear the trucks whining long before they got to her and she was keeping off the highway so as not to be hit from behind. There was a deep median of grass between the lanes and she had been watching the orange tractors for a good while now, the trucks with their flat beds parked and the groups of men in hard hats from a distance.

She had rested for a time just on the edge of the city limits at dawn after asking directions at a gas station just as a man was opening the door. He had pointed, told her to go west to Batesville, then south, and he had gone on in and started turning on the lights. She stood there for a minute, looking around for a hose or a water tap, but there was only the concrete island with the gas pumps and the cubicle of glass with racks of cigarettes and the man sitting there fiddling with the register. So she went on down the street and out to the intersection and started following the highway west, the way he had pointed.

She was very thirsty now and the grass was littered with Styrofoam cups, aluminum cans, shredded pieces of truck tires. She stepped around a crushed armadillo with its shattered shell and hairy legs, the toes splayed on the stones along the roadway. Off to the right she could see some white horses gathered at a trough and drinking from it. One raised its head and shook it mane, then lowered its head again. But she didn't guess she was ready to be drinking from a horse's trough just yet and she kept on walking.

She didn't know if she could walk all day in this heat or not. She had done it before, though never when she was feeling like this. The headache had been steadily climbing up the back of her skull and now it had settled into a place somewhere just behind her eyeballs and it caused her to grind her back teeth together in an effort to keep her jaws clamped tight so that maybe her footsteps wouldn't make her head fly apart.

She could feel the blood jolting in her legs and sometimes she weaved as she walked. What she had seen beyond the door the night before was still running like a fragment of a movie in her head and she could still hear the sounds they had been making. She hadn't known such things could be done, two men with a woman like that, and she wondered now which one was the father of the little child she had held.

The cars kept passing her and even if she'd had her thumb out there was no place for them to pull over except for the places where side roads entered the main highway. She could see houses set back from the blacktop but no people moved in the yards. She was closer to the orange trucks now and she could see the mowers canted up on the hillsides and a thin stream of shorn grass and weeds spraying out behind the tractor, a cascade of green bits and pieces.

She waited until the road was clear, then stepped out into

the highway and walked across the center line and down into the grass of the median and went toward the orange tractors again She could hear them now, the diesel chug and the steady swish of the Bush Hog and she could see the black smoke jetting from the pipe as the driver turned to make another pass. The trucks were parked in a flat turnaround between the two sections of road and a few men were loading portable signs printed with large block letters MOWERS AHEAD and the cars kept whizzing by on the road above her, her head about level with the pavement now, walking through the clipped grass and the torn bits of aluminum from the shredded cans and here and there jagged bits of glass she had to watch for, the soles of her tennis shoes so thin now and not able to turn away something as sharp as that.

The men climbed into the truck and it pulled away, one man riding on the side step, a red light flashing on a dome mounted in the roof. The tractor climbed out of the wide ditch and went along the shoulder against the traffic until it had gone past the turnaround and then it swerved down and once more the grass began to fly out behind it.

An air horn blared on the road above her and she looked up at the moving face of an older man watching her from his high cab. The truck changed gears without slowing and rolled on. A car passed it. There was not one bit of shade now and the sun beat down on her shoulders and the top of her head. She swung the strap of the purse up on her shoulder and kept walking. The orange truck had gone ahead and she couldn't see it anymore. There was just the man on the tractor still mowing. He went at a slow pace, back and forth in narrow sweeps, ever deeper into the grass valley until he too went from sight and there was just the exhaust pipe with the smoke drifting from it to show her his location. He cross to the other side and she saw him start making his passes, climbing steadily toward the road.

She stopped and sat down on the side of the hill and hung

her head between her arms and her knees. Her breath was coming hard and a tick was crawling on her ankle. She picked it off, tried to rub it off her finger, finally flicked it away with her nail. The thing about catching a ride was that you never could tell who was going to pick you up. If they stopped and you didn't like their looks, then you had to tell them to go on, that you didn't want to ride after all. She saw that she was going to have to be careful of boys now and that she'd been lucky the night before. And then sometimes they'd cuss you if you didn't get in with them after they'd stopped, call you a bitch or whore or say *Fuck you, then*, or throw gravel on your legs when they spun off from the side of the road.

She didn't want to keep sitting there and she didn't want to go on. The tractor had climbed out of the ditch once more and it was going over the hill where the truck had gone and in another minute she couldn't see any of them. Fay knew they had water. Men who worked in the sun all day had to have water.

She wished she'd taken a few extra cigarettes from the pack on the dash of the truck last night. She didn't have any now. She'd already looked through her purse, hoping, but she'd known there weren't any more in there before she'd even looked. And they cost more than a dollar. She thought they cost about a dollar and a half.

Another horn blew at her up on the road, kept blowing, faded away down the highway and then it stopped blowing and she could hear the rush of its tires on the pavement. Far away down the country in front of her the road curved into the distance of a pale green mass that lay at the edge of the sky and that sky was the lightest blue she had ever seen, almost without color, and in the emptiness one small black form drifted with wide wings spread, turning in the currents, riding loops down and then lifting, stalling for a moment before it rushed downward again She looked up at the buzzard and muttered, "You gonna have to wait a while if you waitin on me."

\* \* \*

She almost didn't hear the car for the noise of the other vehicles on the road, but she turned her head from where she was sitting on the edge of the grass and saw a set of wheels slowing to a stop behind her, pebbles embedded in the treads, and then she looked up at the whole car and saw who was driving it and her heart sank fast. She stood up quickly, brushing at the back of her skirt.

The trooper stopped the car in the center of the turnaround and picked up the radio mike and said something into it and then he was getting out, reaching back in for his hat, and she saw the black tips of his boots coming out from behind the door. Then he was standing there with his neatly pressed gray trousers, a blue stripe down each leg, a gun on his hip and a crisp shirt, his nameplate and his shiny brass and all the authority she feared. He put the hat on and then his face was in shade.

She could see the short dark hair just under the rim of the hat and his clean-shaven cheeks where tiny red vessels had come to the surface of his skin and her own distorted face twinned in the sunglasses with the cars on the other highway passing into and out the other side of the little gold rims. He touched the brim of his hat with his fingers, nodded.

"Can I help you, ma'am," he said.

"I don't know," she said. "I was just out walkin. I ain't done nothing wrong have I?"

"I don't guess." He glanced up at the sky for a moment. "Mighty hot for a stroll. You headed somewhere in particular?"

She didn't know anything about cops except that they rousted you from the park benches and stared at you when they saw you walking down the road. And sometimes they pulled over and asked you where you were going, like this one. She didn't want to say the wrong thing. She knew he had all the power.

"I'm headed to Biloxi," she said. "I was just settin here. I got hot. I wanted to rest a little."

The radio chattered loudly inside the cruiser but he didn't pay any attention to it He was as good-looking a man as she'd ever seen and she wondered how old he was. She put a little tease in her voice, trying it out. She was loose now. She could talk to men now. She didn't think she wanted any boys.

"You ain't gonna arrest me, are you?"

"I don't reckon so," he said. "You feeling okay?"

She wasn't, but she didn't want to tell him that. He might take her somewhere, do something with her.

"It sure is hot," she said. "I wanted to catch up with them fellers to get some water if they had some but I can't catch up with em."

"Who?"

She pointed. The road crew was nothing but a knot of men with a truck beside them, vague and hazy through the heat.

"They been cutting the grass but I can't catch up with em. I thought I could but I've done about give out. That's why I was settin down."

She looked up at him but could read nothing on his face. He seemed to be waiting for something else.

"I didn't know whether to try and catch a ride with somebody or not," she said. "I don't know who to trust and who not to."

He watched her and didn't say anything. Then he turned and leaned into the car and picked up the radio mike again He took off his hat and tossed it onto the front seat beside some papers and a clipboard. She could see a shotgun in a steel rack behind the seat, a steel mesh divider in back. He said something into the mike and waited for an answer, and somebody replied, a woman's voice, and he spoke into it again and then hung it back on the dash. There were handcuffs on his wide belt and she could see the imprint of his wallet in his back pocket. When he came out he was taking the cap off a plastic bottle of water, which he handed to her.

"Here," he said. "You'll get dehydrated out in this sun."

She turned a drink down her throat and felt it come alive again, and swallowed and swallowed again, and took it down and gasped for air, and then turned it up again and then it was all gone. The bottle was light, almost weightless in her hand. She gave it back to him.

"Thank you," she said, and wiped her mouth. "That was mighty good."

He tapped the bottle against his leg and looked down the road, just a glance, and then he turned back to her.

"My car's got an air conditioner in it. Why don't you get in and sit down for a while?"

She was almost afraid to get in, but she figured she'd better do what he said.

"Okay. Yes sir"

He walked around with her, opened the door on the opposite side, and she looked in and stopped. He leaned in and pushed it all over to his side and got back out of her way. She sat down and was enveloped in a waft of cold air. He shut the door on her and she sat with her purse in her lap.

The glass was tinted and now the outside world was not bright and hot like it had been, He got in on the other side and buckled his seat belt and told her to put hers on and she looked down at meaningless straps until he saw that she didn't know how to do what he was talking about and bent toward her, his arm brushing against her, pulled the strap across her without touching her again and fastened it into the holder on the seat.

"There," he said. He reached up for the shifter and then

stopped. He slumped back against the seat, tapped his fingers on the steering wheel. He took a pack of cigarettes from his shirt pocket and when he saw her looking at them, shook one loose from the pack and offered it. She took it and said thank you again.

He pushed in on the lighter on the dash and looked across the road at the newly clipped grass.

"Are you in trouble with somebody?"

"I don't reckon so," she said. "I just didn't want to stay where I was at."

The lighter popped out and he reached for it, held the burning red coil up to her and she bent her face holding the cigarette with her fingers until it was lit. He lit his own and rolled the window down six inches. The car looked and smelled brand new and except for the papers on the dash it was very clean. She couldn't even hear it running.

"This sure is a nice car," she said.

He turned his head a bit when she said that. He seemed amused for a moment.

"You ever rode in one of these before?"

She took that to mean had she ever been arrested. She cracked the window and tipped her ashes out, but they blew back into the car. She fanned at them.

"Don't worry about that," he said.

"I don't want to mess up your car."

"It's not mine. I just use it for a while and then they give me another one. You never have rode in one?"

"No sir. I never have been in no trouble."

"Why are you out walking down the road?"

She looked down at her lap. The cars were going slower on the highway now. The only reason she was scared to tell him the truth was because she was afraid he might take her back and as close as she could figure she'd only made it about fifteen miles maybe. In twenty minutes she could be right back.

"I left because of my daddy," she said.

He relaxed in the seat and she studied him. There was a wedding band on his left hand and there were some fresh scratches on his right forearm, tiny black lines scabbed in little arcs.

"And you're headed to Biloxi?"

"Yes sir. They said it was a long way. But I heard it was nice down there. They supposed to have a beach and all."

"Who said?"

"Some boys that picked me up last night."

"Some boys? Where'd they pick you up at?"

"It was on this road close to where I used to live."

"Did you know these boys?"

"No sir. I didn't know em. They just stopped and picked me up."

She could tell he was getting agitated but she didn't know why. Maybe he could tell that she'd been drinking the night before. Or maybe she was keeping him from doing his work.

"How many boys?"

"It was three of em. They had this boat in the back of their pickup and they had a big mess of fish they'd caught."

"And you didn't know them"

"I didn't know em from Adam."

And that made him mad. He nodded and she saw a muscle flex in his jaw. He turned his face to the half open window.

"How'd you know they wouldn't kill you?"

"They didn't look like they would."

He turned to look into her eyes.

"Have you any idea how dangerous it is for a girl like you to be out on this road at night? Or any road. There's people that drive around just looking for somebody hitching a ride."

She put her hands in her lap and looked out the windshield.

"I was tired of walkin," she said. "I didn't know where I

was and I'd done almost got dogbit one time already. I didn't think they was gonna try to hurt me."

She thought back to what she had seen them doing in that room. He kept looking out the window for a while. He took a few more drags off the cigarette and then flipped it out and rolled up the window.

"You're headed west, right?"

"I guess so," she said. "They said go west and then south. What's the name of that place where you turn off? Batesville?"

"Yeah," he said. "That's where my office is. I ain't supposed to be giving rides but I guess I can take you that far if you want to go."

"Well," she said. "If you don't care."

He picked up the radio mike and told them that he was 10-8 again and looked both ways before he turned the car around. She tossed her smoke out and rolled up the window.

"That air too cool on you?" he said.

"It's fine."

He waited until the road was clear and then the power in the motor pressed her back in the seat and they were running down the hill in the cool air and the world was softened and diffused and she felt that they were floating on a cushion of air, rushing headlong toward those distant hills and the green line of trees slightly shimmering beneath that awful sun.

* * *

His name was Sam Harris and he told her he was forty-two years old. His home was at Cole's Point, he said, a lakeside house on the reservoir at Sardis, and he got to telling her about crappie fishing and running trotlines for White River cats and deer hunting in the deep hollows of hardwood timber on the forty acres he owned. There was just him and his wife now, he said, and she liked gardening, and had some clubs she belonged to, but he said he liked to fish a lot and she didn't.

At the Sonic in Batesville he pulled in and bought lunch for her, a thick hamburger with melted cheese and pickles, fries, and a Coke in a tall cup, her cheeks stuffed and chewing when he pulled back out into traffic and turned up Highway 51. Out past the high school and into the country land where the cotton was growing and the rusted irrigators crept on their wheels spraying water over the sunburned rows and past deserted silos with their conical roofs punched in, the rotten boards hanging and crumbling down the sides.

Fields of tall corn with the tasseled tops swaying in the wind and old barns where black cows lay chewing their cuds inside new pipe fences. Climbing back into the hills and turning northeast toward Highway 4 and the fronds of kudzu that had crawled unceasingly to the sides of the road and held out their trembling vines to the air. Back down again to 7 south of Holly Springs, his district, he said, pretty big district, wasn't it? And then again among the lumbering trucks so docile and slow now with him behind them, their broad polished backs shining until they passed them and left them behind, the car always kept at a swift and steady gait that seemed to sweep everything before them past, as if there were some purpose to their travel, a certain destination, but he said that he was just cruising.

Once in a while he would flash his lights at an oncoming car after reading numbers in red from a machine mounted on the dash but he didn't pull anybody over.

The sun went slowly across the sky until it hung straight overhead and invisible, glaring down on the roadway and always the cars and trucks climbing and passing, trailing one another in a line. He let Fay out to use the bathroom at a barbecue joint just north of Lafayette County and when she got back in the cruiser he handed her an ice-cold bottle of lemonade and a BC Powder and after another ten miles she felt lots better.

With her stomach full and the cool bottle sitting in her lap and the window cracked to let the smoke out, she started telling him about her life up till now.

The wind sucked the smoke from the car as farms and houses rolled by and treelines appeared and gradually grew closer and then passed as new ones appeared far down the road. He drove without speaking and she felt by then that he wasn't going to make her go back home. They were almost back to the place where he had picked her up when she started telling him about the two times her father had crept up on her in the dark, how he'd ripped her clothes and put his hand around her throat and tried to choke her down, and of how she'd fought and kicked and scratched at his eyes until she was able to get away from him almost naked and run into the woods to hide, alone with the night birds and the tree frogs calling and her heart hammering finally slower inside her chest.

She told him about her little sister, Dorothy, and how she had just stopped talking a long time ago, and about Gary, her brother, who had worked all summer and kept them from starving, and how, yesterday evening she had told her mother she was leaving and had walked out of the yard.

It was midafternoon by then. He slowed down and then turned off the highway onto an asphalt road where signs advertised boat rentals and lots for sale, a state park with symbols for camping and boating. He took his time on this road, following the curves and hills where the grass had been neatly mowed and young trees had been planted. He drove for a couple of miles and they came to the near end of the great levee where short treated posts held lengths of chain stretched down both sides. Out across the bright water she could see boats moving across the waves, specks of blue and white and red that were other boats far out on the lake. And there were sharp-winged birds soaring in the air, flocks of them that lifted and turned, and when she rolled her window down she could hear their voices on the wind.

Sam slowed the car and drove along the levee for a while. He smiled some, looking out at it.

"Pretty, ain't it?"

"It sure is," she said. "I ain't never see than much water before."

"It used to be the biggest earthen dam in the world. Then I think they built a bigger one over in Iran or Iraq one. Most of this one was built with mule power. Back in the thirties. You want to get out and look at it?"

"I'd like to go swimmin in it," she said. "If I knew how to swim."

He grinned and pulled the car over to an observation point and parked it close to the chains and left it running. They got out. He walked around to the front of the car and put his hands in his pockets and leaned against a lamppost that was there, watching her.

"There's a beach on the other side," he said, turning his head toward the lower lake. She looked down there at the groves of trees and the picnic tables, tents and campers under the trees.

"This is nice," she said. She was smiling. She stepped over the chain and stood there looking out across the water. It was out there as far as she could see.

"And you say you live over here?"

He came over to where she was and stopped beside her, stretched his hand and arm out and pointed to the south side.

"You can't see it from here," he said. "I mean you can't see the house, hardly. I can see this levee from my back deck. I go out there in the morning to drink my coffee. It's over there behind that bluff you can see there, where that red dirt is."

She nodded, looking, trying to see it. It was cool there with the wind coming off the water and the boats rocking up and down on the waves.

"What are you going to do?" he said. He sat down on the

post next to her and folded his fingers together, watching the water move.

"I don't know." She turned to look at him. "I guess I'll just head south. I don't know what else to do. I don't want to go back."

His voice was quiet and he kept his fingers locked together. He drew in a deep breath.

"How will you live, though? What will you do for money? For food? And a place to stay. You can't just sleep on the side of the road. Somebody'll do something to you. It happens to young girls all the time. I've seen it." He turned to look at her. "I've seen it myself, with my own eyes."

Down below them there was a slanting wall of big white rocks that went all the way down to the water that lapped against them and receded, was unending in its movement.

"I guess I'll try to find a job," she said.

"But you'd have to find a place to stay. You can't sleep in a park, the cops'll roust you in any town you go to. Or they'll take you to a shelter. They might even send you back to where you came from. There's no telling what might happened to you."

She looked down at her dirty fingernails and the nails of both her big toes sticking through the ragged tennis shoes. She knew she looked bad and she wished there was something she could do about it.

"What you think I ought to do?"

Sam got up from the post and put his hands back in his pockets. The wind was whipping the legs of his trousers and the radio was chattering inside the cruiser.

"I think you ought to come home with me and let me and my wife fix you some supper. You like steak?"

She gave him a small smile.

"I'd like to try it."

"Come on, then," he said.

She gazed out over the water and saw that today was

better than yesterday, and decided to go with it. She got up and they walked back to the car.

\* \* \*

The drive that led to his house curved through a big stand of mature pines. You couldn't see the house from the main road, he told her. The cruiser nosed along the drive and the trees were close on each side.

"Amy's probably out on the deck with her nose stuck in a book. We can take you swimming after while if you want to go."

She didn't know what to expect here. She'd never imagined that a cop would have a house in the woods or like to fish.

"I might get in if it ain't in the deep. I ain't never had a chance to learn how to swim."

"Everybody needs to know how to swim," he said. "What if you were on a boat and it sank? You ever thought about that?"

"I ain't never been on a boat."

He slowed down going around the last curve and she caught a glimpse of the house then, a flash of tall windows and cypress siding, a high peaked roof.

"You hang around me very long you'll be on one."

The drive went over a low wooden bridge and when he pulled up and stopped in front of the house, she could do nothing but look at it for a minute. It seemed to have grown in one piece out from the side of the hill, the entire side wall made of glass so that she could see the furniture inside and fans turning in the ceiling and potted plants hanging from big wooden beams. The old pines that grew beside it covered it in a deep shade and littered its top with their needles. A wide deck ran all across the back of it and there were padded lounging chairs and tables and past the corner of the deck she could see the water of the lake rippling out there.

"This is your house?" she said.

"Home sweet home," he said, opening the door He had already checked out on the radio and he grabbed his notebook and got his keys. "Come on in and we'll find Amy. I know she's probably got a swimming suit you can wear."

Her fingers went to the door handle but they were slow in opening it. He was standing in front of the car, waving her in with his keys. She opened the door and got out, still looking up at the house. Now she was even more ashamed of her town tennis shoes, the blouse and the skirt that were too small for her. She shut the door and walked up beside the fender and stopped. Sam had already gone ahead to the steps and now he turned to look back at her.

"Well? You coming in or what?"

"You sure it's all right?" she said. "You don't think your wife will get mad or nothing?"

He walked back to her and gently took one of her hands.

"Come on, Fay," he said. "It's all right."

She followed him then, the two of them hand in hand going up the steps to the door that was mostly glass too and inside to the clean pine floors and the big stone fireplace and the stuffed animal heads and fish hanging on the walls. The fans turned overhead and she could see a big kitchen and a butcher block table under a rack of copper pans and utensils,

"There she is," he said, and he turned loose of her hand and set his things on a table in the corner. "Let's go out on the deck."

She didn't know what to do with her purse so she just held on to it, He didn't wait for her but went to the double glass door and pushed one side of it back and stepped out. A small woman in shorts and T-shirt who looked a lot like him sat in her chair with a drink in her hand. A book lay open and facedown on the table. He said something to her and pointed back inside and she got up a little unsteady and then they both came back inside.

The woman smiled at Fay and sipped her drink. Her black hair was streaked with bits of gray and she had pretty white teeth, bright brown eyes that seemed shy and careful. She came forward with her hand out, and she seemed to Fay no more than a girl herself. Then when Fay looked closer at her eyes she saw the tight wrinkles of skin that makeup couldn't hide.

"Amy," Sam said, "this is Fay. I've asked her to eat supper with us tonight."

Fay turned loose of her purse with one hand and took the hand that was offered.

"Hey Fay." Her hand was limp and cool, fragile as a bird's wing. It felt like it had no strength at all.

"Hey," she said. She could feel her face turning red. She shook the hand quickly and released it, and then looked at Sam for what to do next.

"I told her we might take her swimming. You got me some beer iced down?"

"It's out on the deck. Why don't you come on out and let's sit down, Fay."

"I'm gonna go change clothes," Sam said, and he went past them unbuttoning his shirt and vanished somewhere in the house. But this Amy was still smiling at her.

"There's a good breeze out here," she said. "It's been awful hot today, hasn't it?"

"Yes ma'am. It sure has."

She followed Amy out the door and watched her slide it shut behind them and then followed her across the deck, watching her walk very carefully.

"Let's sit down over here in the shade, Fay. Would you like a cold Coke or something?"

Amy took a seat in a rocking chair and Fay sat down on the bench that ran along the railing of the deck.

"Yes ma'am. That'd be real nice."

There was an ice chest between them and Amy opened the lid and reached into it and pulled out a can and handed it to her.

"Thank you."

"You're welcome. Sam's working the day shift now and he always wants a cold beer when he gets home. So I always have some iced down for him. Are you hungry? Would you like something to eat?"

Fay shook her head and opened the can.

"No ma'am. I'm fine, thank you. He bought me a hamburger a while ago. Best one I ever had."

She still had her purse in her lap but she picked it up now and set it beside her feet and held the can with both hands. She smiled, looked down, took a drink of the Coke. Something unexpected happened in her throat and two spurts of it shot out of her nose, fizzing spots that landed on her skirt. She jumped up and wiped at her skirt and then at her nose, sidestepping, her face blushing hotly.

"Goddamn," she said. "I didn't mean to do that." She paused and looked up. "I'm sorry. I didn't mean to say that either. I'm just nervous."

Amy had already stepped to a table and pulled a paper towel off a roll there. She was still smiling when she moved up close and dabbed at the wet spots.

"Nothing to worry about," she said. "I had a date with this boy one time and we'd been swimming, went in this beer joint to get some ribs and I sat down on this chair and farted in my wet swimming suit and you could hear it all over the room."

She stepped back and winked. "Shit happens. Don't worry about it. Would you rather have a beer?"

Fay looked at the Coke in her hand and already she knew that she liked what was in the brown bottles better.

"I guess so," she said.

"Or I can mix you a drink. I like Ruby Red grapefruit

juice and Stoly. You ever drink that?"

"Nome. A beer's fine," she said.

Amy got one and opened it after a few tries and handed it to her. They sat back down and Amy picked up her glass. She looked into it for a second and took a sip, looked out across the lake, and then her eyes moved back to Fay.

"We don't get much company out here. We're a couple of regular hermits. I go to the beauty shop and the grocery store. That's it, beauty shop, grocery store, over and over."

"It sure is nice out here," Fay said. "I ain't never seen such a pretty house."

"It's too big," Amy said. "Too much to clean."

Fay tucked her feet under the bench so that her tennis shoes were hidden. She wished she had some better ones,. The beer was very cold when she sipped from it.

"All this water," she said, "I'd love to live out here."

Amy nodded and leaned back, holding her drink with both hands. She crossed her ankles.

"I don't never go out on it. It's pretty to set and look at, though." She took another drink and looked back up. "He likes to fish. He goes out on it a lot." She studied the lake for a while. "Yeah. A lot," she said, and then she lifted the glass as if that explained something. She gave Fay a weak smile. "I like to relax when I get off from work."

Fay just smiled and bobbed her head and tried to think of something to say to her. She wanted Sam to come on back out now. But looking at the water was nice. She could have sat there and looked at it for a long time. It made her feel good. The water made her feel like she belonged beside it in some old familiar way.

Now that she was so close, Amy looked older than him. By a good bit.

Fay peeled at the label on her beer and then made herself stop. Little fritters of paper to pick up.

"I was afraid of him when he first stopped," she said. "I

was afraid he was gonna arrest me or something. I'd done walked a long ways and I was wore out. But he gives me a ride and bought me a hamburger. He's a nice man."

"Yes," Amy said uncertainly. "A very nice man."

"How long y'all been married?"

Amy picked at something on her shirt and looked back up.

"This year makes twenty-one years," she said. "We got married right out of college and he went to work for the highway patrol. We've lived all over but we're from Verona, over close to Tupelo He got transferred a couple of times and we lived in Natchez for a while, stayed in Lucedale for a couple of years, had a house in Grenada for a year or so. We have a house in Batesville for eight years and then we built this one. He loves it out here, fishes every day it's pretty. You want to see his boats?"

She got up and waked over to the rail and Fay followed her. Amy was pointing down into a cove where there was a wooden dock. Two boats drifted on their ropes. One was a big shiny thing with a big outboard motor and the other one was a scratched and dented old metal one.

"I gave him that old one on our first anniversary," Amy said. "He still uses it to crappie fish. You like fish?"

"I've eat it some," Fay said. She leaned up against the rail and set her beer down carefully on top of it and unpinned her hair and shook it loose. Amy turned and looked at her.

"You've got pretty hair," she said.

"It always looks awful. I can't do nothing with it."

She felt Amy's hand come out and touch the ends of her hair, turned her face just a bit and nervously took another sip of the beer. She wished she had a cigarette.

"It just needs a trim is all," Amy said. "I could trim it if you want me to. That's what I do for a living."

"You do?"

"I'm a beautician. I've got my own shop over at Batesville.

Sam bought it for me a long time ago. But I've got all the stuff in the house to do this I could do it before supper if you want me to."

The hand lingered for a moment and then she pulled it back, reluctantly it seemed. And she moved closer and looked into her eyes.

"Tell me something, Fay."

"What's that?"

The glass door slid open and Sam stepped out onto the deck in blue jeans and a black shirt.

"Y'all having a conference already?" he said. He was happy, though. He looked smaller somehow without his uniform on and Fay began to see now that he was different at home. He pulled out a beer and twisted the top off and put his cigarettes and lighter on the table and then came over to stand beside them against the rail.

"So what you think?" he said. "Is this a little piece of heaven or what?"

"It's nice," Fay said. "It's the nicest place I've ever seen."

"You want to go for a ride in my boat? It's fast, now."

"I don't know." She looked kind of worried. "That water looks deep,"

"I've got some life jackets. I won't let you drown."

He turned his beer up and took a big drink from it. Amy was leaning against the rail, looking toward the house.

"She just got here, Sam. Maybe she wants to rest."

"Oh. Yeah." He nodded and Fay saw something pass across his face, saw something too in the way Amy spoke to him that was just a bit too hard, a bit too weary. He nodded. "Well. Maybe after a while."

Amy walked around him and reached up to touch Fay's hair again with her fingers.

"I told her I'd be glad to trim her hair for her. And I thought she might like a nice hot bath."

"I would like to go for a ride," Fay said quickly. "I sure

would like to get this messy hair of mine fixed, too." She took another drink of her beer. "And a bath sounds good."

It didn't seem to bother him a bit. He stepped over to the table and shook out a cigarette.

"Okay, sure," he said. "I've got some things I can be doing. It's pretty hot to be out in the boat right now anyway. Maybe we can take a ride when it cools off some. Then we'll come back and fix those steaks. How does that sound?"

"That sounds real nice," Fay said. "Can I get a cigarette from you?"

"Help yourself. There's a carton in there on the kitchen table, too."

She got one of the cigarettes and they stood around and talked some more. He was still standing there drinking his beer at the rail when they went into the house. Fay looked back at him and he turned, gave her a wave with the bottle, and she saw him go back to watching the water move under the wind and the limbs of the big old pines swaying in the breeze.

* * *

Amy brought her another beer after she was in the deep tub, stretched out with her toes spread beneath the faucet and her head resting on an inflatable pillow and a mass of fragrant bubbles almost spilling over the side of the tub. The warmth of the water had seemed to soak into her bones and now she was half asleep and wanted nothing more than to lie here forever.

She sat up when Amy came back in and set the beer on the edge of the tub.

"You want some more hot water?" she said.

"No ma'am."

"Stop calling me ma'am. I'm not but forty-one. How old are you?"

Amy put the lid down on the commode and took a seat on it.

"Seventeen," Fay said. "I'll be eighteen in September."

"So you're not out of school yet?"

Fay picked up the beer and looked at it for a second.

"I don't go to school. I ain't in a long time."

"Why not? Did you not like school?"

"I liked it fine when I got to go. But we've moved around a lot. And we all had to work. The last school I had was in the fifth grade. My daddy wouldn't let me go no more after that.

Said it was a waste of time and I needed to work and help the family. So that's what I did."

She leaned back against the pillow and sipped on the beer. Amy had crossed her legs and she sat watching her with her hands in her lap.

"Do you still want to go to school?"

"It's too late now. I've done missed so much."

"How's your reading?"

"Not too good. I needed glasses a long time ago but I never did get any. Daddy said they cost too much money. I can read something way off like a road sign but it's hard for me to read a piece of paper. I have to hold it way out. Like this beer bottle. I can read what kind it is but I can't read these little bitty words down here."

She felt like she was talking too much so she slumped back down in the water and looked at the tile wall in front of her. She didn't even know these people and she was telling them all these things. But it was hard not to. Already she knew it was going to be hard to leave here, get back on the highway. Biloxi didn't sound like such a great idea now, now that she'd found this place. Amy was drunk but it was a kind and a soft drunk.

"I've got some clothes I want you to try on after while," Amy said. She got her drink off the sink and turned it up. She lightly stroked her lip with two fingers. "Some things that belonged to my daughter. I bet they'll fit you. I bet they will."

"Thank you," Fay said. "I could sure use some more clothes. What, did she just outgrow em."

"She doesn't need them anymore," Amy said. She got up from where she was sitting. She had already hung some clean underwear and some jeans and a blouse on a rack on the wall. "I'll lock this door on my way out so Sam won't accidentally walk in on you. You stay in here as long as you want. Then you can take that boat ride with him before we eat if you want to. Okay?"

"Okay. Thank you."

Amy stepped out. Fay leaned back into the warm water and lifted the beer again and tilted a long cool drink down her throat. Oh yeah, it was going to be hard to leave this place.

* * *

IF YOU ENJOYED THIS BOOK, WE ENCOURAGE YOU
TO READ THE FIRST VOLUME IN OUR ANTHOLOGY
SERIES: *MOJO RISING: MASTERS OF THE ART,
EDITED BY JAMES L. DICKERSON*

Authors include:

William Faulkner                    Eudora Welty

Stark Young                         Tennessee Williams

Elizabeth Spencer                   Richard Wright

Ellen Gilchrist                     Willie Morris

Shelby Foote                        Ellen Douglas

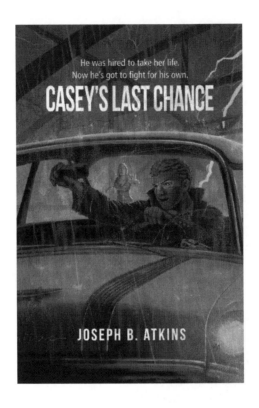

"Joe Atkins's *Casey's Last Chance* is such pitch-perfect vintage noir, you can almost smell the cigarette burning in the ashtray, a woman's perfume drifting past. With a twisty plot, vibrant characters, and hardboiled grit to burn, it's everything you want in a crime novel."—**Megan Abbott, Edgar-award-winning author of *Dare Me* and *The Fever***